Happily Never After

Sudeep Nagarkar

First published by Westland Publications Private Limited in 2021

1st Floor, A Block, East Wing, Plot No. 40, SP Infocity, Dr MGR Salai, Perungudi, Kandanchavadi, Chennai 600096

Westland and the Westland logo are the trademarks of Westland Publications Private Limited, or its affiliates.

ISBN: 9789391234348

10 9 8 7 6 5 4 3 2 1

Typeset by SÜRYA, New Delhi
Printed at Thomson Press India Ltd.

Prologue

Being in love gives you a sense of belonging but gathering the courage to confess that love gives you anxiety. It's like holding a burp in for a long time. You wonder if holding it in will make the feeling go away, but do it for too long and it begins to hurt. She had a similar strong urge. Not to burp, but to confess her feelings to someone she loved with all her heart!

'You really think I have taken the right decision?' she asked. 'What if ...'

'If you ask me, you have no choice,' Nisha said. She took a sip of her black coffee and went to stand beside her friend in the balcony of their apartment.

The city had gone to sleep under a blanket of darkness, unaware of the tornado of emotions she was going through. She was caught up in thoughts that swirled and raced around in her mind. She wanted to express her love to the one who had stolen her heart; she wanted to tell him how she felt around him. But she was unsure if she should be the one to initiate the conversation.

Seeing the anxiety in her eyes, Nisha said, 'Look, I know that falling in love is the most wonderful feeling, but you should also be with that person you love. For that, one of you needs to propose to the other at some point in time.'

'I don't know ... I feel I should not look as if I'm desperate to be with him.' She felt that if a girl chased the love of her life, she may be considered chaalu or some such thing.

'That's ridiculous. This patriarchal society has made you feel that way. If a guy does the same thing, he is considered sweet and romantic. Why can't a girl stand up for her love and express her feelings? Who are others to judge you and tell you to stay within society's defined limits? To hell with society's norms. Just listen to your heart.'

But it wasn't that easy for her. Her mindset was influenced by her hometown, the place she had spent most of her life, and what she had seen around her. A small town in Madhya Pradesh. Even in college, there were girls who, despite liking someone, never confessed their love until the guy approached them. They kept their feelings to themselves to avoid getting tagged as a 'loose character' or 'easily approachable' or someone with no integrity. And the ones who did and faced rejection were also labelled.

'If a guy gets rejected by a girl then nobody bats an eyelid, but if a girl gets rejected by a guy, then all hell breaks loose. That's why I am unsure if I should ...'

Happily Never After

Sudeep Nagarkar has authored fourteen bestselling novels: *Few Things Left Unsaid, That's the Way We Met, It Started With a Friend Request, Sorry You're Not My Type, You're the Password to My Life, You're Trending in My Dreams, She Swiped Right Into My Heart, All Rights Reserved for You, Our Story Needs No Filter, She Friend Zoned My Love, The Secrets We Keep, Stand By Me!, A Second Chance* and *Can't Quarantine Our Love*. He has been featured on the Forbes longlist of the most influential celebrities for two consecutive years. He was also awarded the 'Celebrity author of 2013' by Amazon and, in 2016, he was awarded the 'Youth Icon of the Year' by Zee Awards and WBR group.

He has given guest lectures at various organisations and institutes, including TEDx and the IITs.

Connect with Sudeep via:
Instagram: sudeepnagarkar
Facebook Fan page: facebook.com/sudeepnagarkar
Facebook Profile: facebook.com/nagarkarsudeep
Twitter: sudeep_nagarkar

'You are not an "abla nari" who's not allowed to take her own decisions. You are an independent working woman, and this is not Jabalpur, it's Pune. No one gives a damn here. At the end of the day, someone, be it he or you, has to take the initiative and express their feelings. After all, all that matters is love.'

Nisha's words comforted her to some extent, yet the turbulence in her head didn't calm down. Even in bed, she could hardly sleep thinking about what she would actually say to him. He had made a special place for himself in her heart, and she had started to build hopes on the foundation of 'what if we could be together'. She didn't want that tower of hope to collapse as she had absolutely no idea how she would deal with it. For a minute, she closed her eyes and said to herself, *Just do it. Take a long breath, don't think of anything, just go to him and say what's in your heart.*

The next minute her eyes were wide open. *But ... how?* She tossed and turned, thinking about *HOW*.

Should I go on my knees? No, that would be too cheesy. Should I give him a ring? No, isn't that a boy thing to do? Then what? Should I leave a letter at his work station? No, what if someone else reads it? Should I take him out for dinner? No, it would be too costly, and anyway the salary isn't credited yet. Should I do it Karan Johar-movies style? No, who will wear all those heavy clothes and run towards him, and anyway our office floor isn't a runway.

Without an answer, she fell asleep. She loved him so intensely that she didn't want to lose him. She loved the feeling of being in love with him and didn't want to let it go. That's why she preferred to love him silently.

The next morning she reached office determined to propose to him. She and Nisha entered the lift along with other people, and Juhi's heart melted. There he was! Abhay! He was looking dapper in formals, his face covered with a slight stubble. He entered the lift just before the doors closed, and Nisha quickly stepped out and winked at her. The lift was crowded, but she could see only him.

Act normal, she said to herself. *What should I say? I need to practice my lines before I say anything.* In her mind, she rehearsed what she was going to say. *'Abhay, I wanted to say something ... Abhay, I love you.'* She kept repeating the lines over and over again until there were only three of them left in the lift. She checked the floor number the other guy had pressed.

Damn, only we three are left and this guy will get off on the seventh floor, and then it's just us in the lift. Just the thought of it is giving me butterflies.

Her nervousness increased with every floor. If Abhay had turned to look behind, he would have sensed there was something terribly wrong with this girl.

Seventh floor. The lift beeped.

There he goes! It was only the two of them now. Her heart was pounding.

'Hi Abhay ...' she finally managed to say.

He looked up from his phone, which he'd been occupied with since he'd entered the lift. He said warmly, 'Good morning! How are you doing?'

'Good, good,' she replied hesitantly and then recited her lines. 'Actually, Abhay, since the last few days, I've been wanting to say something to you.'

Abhay took a step closer to her and, looking in her eyes, said, 'I know what you want to say.'

She froze for a second, she didn't know how to react. She forgot what she been practising completely and stood speechless, her eyes locked on his. All she could say was, 'Really?'

Abhay held her hand and said, 'Yes, and I feel the same for you.'

A thousand-volt current passed through her body and she shivered. Her heart jumped with joy and a smile appeared on her face. 'Oh, Abhay, I love you so much.'

'I love you too.'

And then he hugged her. It felt surreal, a miracle. It was a touch she had pined for, for so long. The musky fragrance of his perfume surrounded her. The rush of emotions she had in that moment couldn't be explained in words. She wanted to hold him forever.

Fourteenth floor. The lift beeped again and she came to reality. She was still standing behind him and as soon as the door opened, he stepped out. She wanted to stop him and tell him how much she loved him, but only gazed after him as he walked into the office.

Nisha had reached the floor in a different lift by now and rushed up to ask, 'What happened? Did you tell him?'

'No, I didn't, I can't. Not today at least.' She started walking towards the office entrance.

'Damn, what's wrong with you?' Nisha said, frustrated.

'Nothing. Today isn't the right day.'

'All of sudden you got this realisation, right?

'Ya, I checked the horoscope for today and it says my love life is complicated and I should not take any major decisions today.'

'Wow, looks like you are never going to talk to him in this lifetime. If you leave it up to these two-rupee horoscope guys, you will stay atmanirbhar for the rest of your life.'

'Whatever,' she said, and walked into the office.

One

'It's seven o'clock. Good morning.'

Juhi was awakened from a deep sleep by Alexa's voice. She had gifted it to herself on her last birthday, and since then she had become entirely dependent on it for her reminders. So much so that she carried it whenever she went for her office trips. But now she was home for Diwali and didn't need to wake up early. She dismissed the alarm but her sleep was disturbed, so she decided to take a jog without informing anyone at home.

She got ready and headed outside. Turning the corner of her street, she saw many familiar faces. Her dad was the third generation in the family to stay in their house, and thus everyone around knew them. On a different sort of day, Juhi could have told you all the things that had happened to her on this route: where her father had taught her to ride a cycle, where her neighbours would give her and her brother Suyash the mawa bati that they loved, the famous stall where she and her friends would eat poha jalebi in the morning.

She jogged for half an hour, listening to her favourite songs. When she returned, she saw her parents were already dressed up for the festival.

'It's Diwali and you are roaming the streets in a tracksuit?' her mom yelled in despair. She had given up trying to make Juhi understand what it meant to be a girl.

'Maa, what do you expect? Do you want me to jog in a saree or salwar-kameez?'

'Why do you have to go and jog in the first place?' her mother said as she sat down on a sofa. She continued in a cribbing tone, 'What will our neighbours think if they see you wearing such clothes? And if you are roaming around like this here, I am sure you would be wearing just minimal clothes in Pune. Beta, who will marry you?'

Juhi turned to her dad. 'Papa, please tell her not today. I am here just for four days.'

Her father indicated with his eyes that she should calm down and gestured to her to hug her mom.

Juhi was pacified and said, 'Anyway, it's Diwali and we should not fight today at least.' She held her mom tight and sat beside her to calm her down. It was only a matter of time before her mom had a smile back on her face.

Later, Juhi and her mother were taking rangoli dabbas from a cupboard when Suyash came out of his room.

'Didi, how am I looking?' he said, checking his white kurta in a mirror again.

'Handsome and dashing as always. Where are you going?'

'Bike rally like every year. You know that we celebrate Diwali by arranging a rally across the town.'

'I know very well the intentions behind it. You guys just want to check out the girls wearing festival outfits as they make rangolis outside their houses.'

'Okay, bye Didi. Bye Maa, Papa,' Suyash said and rushed out before anyone could react to Juhi's statement. He was a couple of years younger than Juhi, and his parents tended to overlook his actions.

When Juhi and her mom were done with their rangoli, her mother raised the million-dollar question again.

'Juhi, Papa and I have been talking about this for a while now. You are the elder child of this family. We want you to get settled down and marry.'

Oh God, not again, Juhi thought. She said, 'Maa, I don't want to get married so soon. Why are you behind me to get married? Even when I call, you have only one topic to talk about, and that's marriage.'

'This time we are not asking you, we are telling you. We have shortlisted the names of boys who are going to come and see you over the next four days. Have a look.' Her mom handed over a paper that had some names on it.

'Is selecting a husband the same as grocery shopping for you? Just go through a list and select the item with the best quality?' As always, she turned towards her father for support. 'Papa please can we keep this for the next time?'

However, her father continued reading the newspaper and didn't respond. Clearly, even he had no say in it.

'Papa, you too.' She sighed. 'Okay then, bring it on.'

• •

The first on the list was Prakash, who visited along with his family that very evening. Juhi looked at him closely, and felt that he had weird expressions like Mr Bean. He was pretending not to look at her but was clearly checking her out. She wanted to reject him outright but for her parents' sake, at their request, she went upstairs to the balcony to chat. She had a similar feeling to how one does while appearing for an interview.

Juhi didn't say a word until he spoke.

'So, your parents were saying that you work in Pune?'

'Yes, do you have a problem with it?' She raised her eyebrows as she offered him tea.

'No … but I feel girls from metro cities are too bold.'

Juhi hadn't expected this and asked him to clarify what he meant. 'Bold, as in?'

'I mean …' He paused, and nervously tried to ask, 'I mean … Did you … you know?'

'You know what? Do you want to ask whether I have had sex or not?' Juhi came straight to his point.

He was flustered and said, 'No, no … I was just asking if you are virgin …'

Means the same thing, dumbass. So, Mr Bean in a matter of a few minutes is turning into Mr Grey. I wish I could kick you right from this balcony.

Juhi gave him a wicked smile. 'No, I am a pro in bed. Do you want to try my wild side? Also, *Fifty Shades of Grey* is my favourite movie. So, we can have BDSM as well after marriage.'

That was it. The speed with which the guy ran away, he would been a definite competitor for a gold medal in the Olympics. The frustration on Juhi's mom's face was evident, but she kept quiet. They wanted her to get married, but they would not force her to go with one of their choices. Her father knew marriage was a big step, and Juhi was his only daughter.

The second on the list, Devesh, visited the next day. He looked quiet and sober. But soon Juhi realised he belonged to the same category of men when he asked, 'Do you know how to cook?'

'Yes, of course,' Juhi replied and asked, 'What about you?'

Devesh reacted as if the question was out of the syllabus for men. He replied, 'Me? Why should I cook? Isn't that a woman's job?'

Wow. Then eating must be a man's job, according to his logic. As if it's written in the Bhagwad Gita. Such morons should be made to cook day and night to know what it takes to be a woman and what 'women's jobs' are! Glad he didn't say that a woman's job is only to give a hand job and a blowjob. Rascal.

'Right, so, what kind of food do you want me to cook after marriage?'

'My mom makes delicious parathas. Even her poha is simply mouth-watering. You can't resist having another serving. Even the best poha jalebi wala is a failure in front of her. And what dal baflas she makes ...'

Juhi couldn't take it anymore. 'So why don't you tell your mom only to cook after marriage? Anyway she too is a woman and sounds like an expert cook.'

This one disappeared quickly too and his parents didn't even bother to call her parents later.

Juhi was fed up with all of it. Only she knew that she was neither outspoken nor had got intimate with anyone. In fact, her nature was totally contradictory to what she had portrayed. She had never even been in a relationship. But her mom felt otherwise.

'I am sure she must be having someone in Pune. Otherwise what is the reason for not accepting such good proposals?' her mother said when they were having their dinner.

'Maa, it's just your imagination—I don't have anyone in Pune. Please let's not discuss this anymore,' she said.

Suyash gestured to Juhi to ignore their mother. He said, 'Maa, if she doesn't want to get married now, why create a fuss? Let her live her life the way she wants.'

Hearing this, Juhi smiled at her younger brother. All these years, they had teased each other, irritated each other but they shared a special bond, and they stood behind each other whenever needed.

'Now, you don't defend your sister. How will we fix your marriage until she gets married? Relieve us also from our responsibilities.'

'How is that connected?' Suyash looked up. 'And anyway, why are you thinking about my marriage already? I have just completed my agricultural engineering.'

'Ya, so? Are you going to support your Papa in his farms or you too want to just run away to some other city like her?' their mother continued her cribbing. She turned towards Juhi's dad to say, 'I had told you not to send her to some other city, but you didn't listen.'

'Enough. Let's have dinner in peace,' he said.

'It's only because of you that they have turned rebellious.' Juhi's mom always had the final say in any argument, and that day was no different.

Later, when Juhi was sitting alone, her dad approached her and sat beside her. He smiled and ran his hand through her hair in affection.

'Are you okay, beta?' he asked.

'Yes, Papa. I am fine.'

'I don't want you to be unnecessarily stressed. I know how hard your work life is. Just relax. No one can force you to get married. You do what your heart says. I am there to support you like always. Make me proud one day.'

'Thanks, Papa.'

'But can I ask you something on a serious note?'

She looked at him and nodded. His presence soothed her every time he had a conversation with her alone. Holding Juhi's hand, her dad asked, 'Do you love someone? If so, then tell us.'

'No, Papa. There's no one in my life. It's just that I want to enjoy my time and the money that I earn before getting married. No restrictions and not being answerable to anyone about my whereabouts.' She paused, smiled and said, 'Except you and mom.'

'Then for my sake, please don't say no to what I ask for.'

'What is it?'

'See, on your mom's insistence, I have spoken to my friend Gupta and asked him to come tomorrow. If things work out between you and his son, then we can take it forward. It's a good family and they too have farms like us.'

'Papa—'

Before she could say more, her dad continued, 'You can reject him if you don't like him, and I promise there won't be a single discussion over it. If I had known previously that you were not prepared yet, I wouldn't have arranged for it. Now please don't say no.'

'Okay, Papa,' Juhi said. She knew her father and was aware that he wouldn't go against her will just for the sake of social pressure.

She wished she could just run away from these marriage prospects, though. *It's not that I don't want to get married, but right now I can't think of any reason to do so. It's my personal choice, and my priorities are different right now. I don't want to hurt my parents, but I just wish they would understand the simple fact that I don't feel it's the right time.*

The next morning, the Guptas dropped in. After an initial conversation, there was no reason to feel that the son Chetan was not better than the others. Juhi tried hard to find a flaw but couldn't. He talked with respect and behaved like a true gentleman. Still, she felt it was too early to judge as she believed that if a guy portrayed himself as Mr Perfect, then there was something fishy about it. It turned out that Juhi wasn't wrong in thinking that way. Once their private conversation was done and they sat along with the families, Chetan showed his true colours.

'I just have one condition,' he said.

'What is it?' Juhi's dad asked.

'Juhi won't work after her marriage. I mean what is the need to do so? We have our farms and, by God's grace, the income from it is sufficient for the family. Also, if we are living in different cities after marriage, then it doesn't make sense.'

'Then you can shift to Pune,' Juhi was quick to respond, as she knew he was digging his own grave.

Chetan was taken aback. 'How can I leave all the work here and shift? Who will handle the farms? After all, tomorrow I would have to look after your farms too, along with Suyash.'

Juhi felt relieved and turned towards her dad with the hope that he would keep his word.

Her dad in a stern voice stated, 'My daughter is my pride and she will continue to work till she wants. No one can stop her from doing so.'

Juhi didn't need to say a word. Her father stood up and requested the Gupta family to leave as he would not want to give his daughter to a family with such regressive thinking.

Afterwards, Suyash teased her, saying, 'Finally you're done with this bunch of proposals. Congratulations for a happy life ahead.'

Her mother was upset as she felt she had lost an opportunity to get Juhi married. Now she would need to wait till the next time she visited from Pune. However, Juhi had a big smile on her face. She was relieved that she had a fighting force standing behind her—the love of her father.

• •

Juhi landed in Pune in the evening the next day after a tiring journey, only to find that her flatmate, Nisha, had changed the lock once again. She was already exhausted with first the bus journey to Jabalpur from her hometown and then a flight to Pune, and Nisha's carelessness irritated her. She pulled out her phone from her handbag and called Nisha.

'Hi Juhi, what's up? Where are you?' Nisha said happily.

'Nisha, I am outside the house and the keys aren't working. You knew I was coming today.'

'Shit, it slipped my mind,' Nisha said.

'As always. You should check with a doctor if you are suffering from short-term memory loss! Anyway, why the hell do you change the lock every time?'

'Darling, you know how our idiot landlord is. He just opens the door without ringing the bell and then yells seeing me with Gautam. Luckily, he has never caught us in an awkward position. I can't change him but I can at least change the lock until he comes back next month to ask for rent, right?'

Juhi had no answer to that. 'Now what am I supposed to do?' she said.

Nisha had a solution for that too. She said, 'I am at J Club, why don't you join me?'

'I am too tired Nisha, please yaar.'

'Come on, you can chill for some time before starting work again tomorrow.'

'And where am I supposed to keep my bags?'

'You can keep it with the guard. He's fond of us—he may lose his phone but not your luggage.' No matter how weird, Nisha always found a solution.

'I don't know how your boyfriend tolerates you,' Juhi said and picked up her bags.

'Come on now, I am waiting,' Nisha said and disconnected the call.

Juhi had no option but to do what her flatmate had suggested. She left her bags with the security guard and took a cab to J Club. When she reached, she saw Nisha sitting with a guy she didn't recognise.

Happy to see her friend after a few days, Juhi forgot about her tiring journey. Nisha's liveliness and energy always refreshed her. They had been flatmates for two years, and they worked in the same office as well—Connecting Dots, a leading marketing firm in the city. From flatmates to good friends had been a journey in itself.

After greeting each other excitedly, Nisha introduced her companion to Juhi. 'Meet my friend Vikas. And Vikas, this is Juhi, my good friend, flatmate and office colleague.'

Then Nisha asked, 'Any drink you would like to order?'

'You know I don't drink,' Juhi replied.

'Darling, I meant non-alcoholic drinks. I know you don't smoke, you don't drink and you are typical marriage material.'

Hearing the word marriage again, Juhi remembered the idiots she had met and narrated the entire story of the past few days. Nisha couldn't hold back her laughter and stated, 'It seems you have returned from the border after winning a war.'

'I feel the same. If Papa had not come to my rescue, Maa would have sent me back along with a husband for sure.'

'Hearing the stories, chances were that you would never return again,' Nisha mocked.

'True that.'

Nisha took a sip of her drink and asked, 'Why does your mom want to get you married so soon? It's the time to focus on a career, have some fun with boys and chill with a few drinks.'

'I wonder what would happen if you stayed at my home for a few days. I am sure you would be the topic of hot gossip for the entire locality, with your attire and outlook towards life.'

Vikas got up to use the rest room, and Juhi leaned towards Nisha and said, 'I've never heard of him in the last couple of years. Since when did he become your friend?'

'It's just been a couple of hours,' Nisha said with a shrug. 'I was bored and came here to have a drink and found him sitting alone. So, you see, two lonely people giving each other company.'

'Ya right. And what about your boyfriend?' Juhi said.

'Flirting increases your lifespan and keeps your heart healthy.'

'Thank god, you didn't become a doctor. Else you would have told every heart patient to flirt.'

'That would be cool. And, by the way, Gautam agrees with it,' Nisha clarified.

'Lucky you,' Juhi exclaimed.

'You too can get lucky, there are a few good-looking guys here. You can try.'

'No, sorry, I am not interested.'

Nisha tried often to get Juhi to date or meet boys, but Juhi always resisted.

'Tell me honestly, are you lesbian? Why do you stay away from boys?'

Juhi was silent for a few seconds and then replied in a low voice, 'Because I've never met someone who can make me fall in love. And I feel no one is even interested.'

Juhi wasn't someone who could be comfortable and friendly with guys in just one interaction, like Nisha. She had started opening up after she moved to Pune, but still felt like she needed to put in a lot of effort. She was innately shy when she had to talk to a guy for the first time, and felt that she would always be like that. But doesn't the flower that is diffident and shy also have a charm? Juhi was like that!

• •

Not much is worse than waking up on a Monday morning after a long weekend and remembering that you have to go back to work. Nisha looked calm, but in her head, she had already killed her boss and other employees. While she kept pressing snooze on her alarm, Juhi had already gotten ready and was done with her morning prayers. That was their everyday routine, and that meant that breakfast was Juhi's duty. She took eggs from the fridge and while they were getting cooked, she called her dad.

'Hi Papa, what's happening?'

'Nothing much. I was about to leave for the market to buy a few items and then will head to the farms. What about you? Ready to leave for work?'

'Almost ...' she tossed the omelette on the plate and put bread in the toaster. 'Papa, is Maa okay now?'

'She will be fine in a couple of days. It's just that she is worried about you and gets stressed. You don't worry.'

'Okay, that's good. Love you, Papa.' Juhi hung up.

Nisha was up by then and was waiting for Juhi to serve her breakfast. The next minute it was in front of her. Nisha took a bite and said, 'I don't know who would have made my breakfast if you hadn't been there. You are a sweetheart. Else this hangover would have killed me.'

'Stop buttering me. Butter the bread instead and get ready ASAP. We are already a few minutes late.'

'Even the team lead allows a few minutes' buffer on Monday,' Nisha said coolly.

However, Juhi insisted on eating quickly, and somehow they reached office in time. When they reached the floor, they bumped into Karan, the team lead. He could make out that Nisha was suffering from a terrible hangover. They were on friendly terms and he was cool so long as team performance was not affected.

'Looks like you had a rocking time last night,' Karan said.

'Just had a couple of drinks more than I should have, Karan,' Nisha replied as she took her seat at her work station.

'Ya, like always.' He made a face and turned towards Juhi whose work station was just next to Nisha's. 'Why don't you instil your qualities at least a little bit in her,' he said in a light tone with his signature smile and left.

'Good morning, Juhi. What's up? How were your holidays?' It was Arpit, their colleague. In some corner of his heart, he liked Juhi, and every morning without fail before starting his work he would make sure to greet her.

Nisha knew how he felt, and knowing Juhi, interrupted. 'She almost had a runaway bride experience. You can ask her later in detail.'

Juhi punched Nisha for making fun of her in front of him.

'Oh really, then why don't we have a coffee break after lunch today? Anyway the client has postponed the delivery date by a couple of days. So, we can relax over a coffee.'

Juhi logged in to her system and said, 'No, sorry, Arpit, I have a lot of pending work today. Sometime later.'

'I don't know when that time is going to come.' Arpit sighed.

Juhi was about to apologise for refusing the offer, but as she raised her head, she saw a new employee walking in. Even though he was a stranger, she felt an element of connection to him. For the first time in her life, she was having such a strong rush of emotions. She watched as he walked towards her and immediately turned away and pretended to work.

He came up to her and said with a smile, 'Hi, I am Abhay. May I know where the HR sits?'

Juhi, break the shackle and at least smile, she said to herself.

But at that moment, the task of stretching her mouth seemed tougher than anything in this world. A basic social habit had completely deserted her. She couldn't understand if it was her core character that was not allowing her to break out of her shyness.

Nisha saw that her friend was unable to respond, so she pointed towards the HR manager's desk. 'There,' she said.

'Thanks,' he said and walked away.

Juhi stared at him while he was having a word with the HR manager. Her heart was as confused as her mind, wondering how a complete stranger could make her feel that way. There was something about him. She didn't know what it was, but she liked the novel sensation she was experiencing.

Two

The heart that's meant to love will develop feelings for someone unexpectedly. You may want to shy away from it but the pull is irresistible. Juhi was in a similar situation. She tried hard not to look at Abhay but had no control over herself. Even when she was working, she couldn't stop herself from gazing over at him. She would try and keep her eyes glued to the computer, but it felt like someone was whispering and asking her to look in his direction. Somehow, she couldn't stop blushing and everything around her slightly blurred and he was the only point of focus.

Why am I so infatuated with him? I have come across many guys in my life but never felt the urge to go and talk with them. Then why do I feel that I should go and talk to this guy? I have seen better looking men than him. Why do I feel that there's something especially attractive about him that's pulling me towards him? Nisha always suggested that I befriend random guys in the club, but I never did, never even felt tempted to. Then why do I feel like befriending you? No, this can't be love. But then, what is it?

Nisha noticed that Juhi was lost in her own world, and when she caught her looking at Abhay a couple of times, she grinned to herself. At lunch break, Nisha called out to Abhay when he was walking towards the cafeteria.

'Why the fuck did you have to call him?' Juhi whispered to Nisha.

'Shut up.'

As he came up to them, Juhi pretended like he didn't exist. She was nervous he would see there was something unusual happening with her.

'Hey, I am Nisha,' she introduced herself to him and said, pretending not to remember his name, 'Sorry, I forgot your name.'

'Abhay. Abhay Diwan,' he said.

'Hi Abhay.' Nisha gave a pleasant smile. 'Nice meeting you. So, are you from Pune or just in the city for work?'

'Been here twenty-six years now.'

A couple of years older, Juhi thought. She pretended like she was messaging someone, looking down at her phone to avoid eye contact with him.

'Where were you working previously?' Nisha's round of questions continued.

'I was working with DL Infotech before, but to be honest, I never enjoyed the work atmosphere there. I feel like it's going to be pleasant in this office with such friendly people around.'

Did he indirectly mention me or was it just a casual statement? Is he also checking me out? No, that can't be true. Juhi's mind was at work.

'So how about treating two friendly people to a coffee.' Nisha grinned and slightly pushed Juhi's hand to tease her.

'Sure, why not?' Abhay said.

No, no ... this is too quick!

'No,' Juhi said loudly all of a sudden. Her reaction startled both of them.

'Are you okay? What happened?' Abhay asked, noticing her fearful face.

'No, I mean, I have got my lunch. I don't want to have coffee right now,' Juhi covered up.

'Oh, okay. Maybe some other time then. Bye!'

Once Abhay left for the cafeteria, Nisha asked Juhi fiercely, 'What is wrong with you? You've been eying him this whole time, and now when he was ready to go have a coffee, you said no?'

'Who said I was eying him? I was totally occupied in my work. Don't make up things.'

'So, you want to play the role of an innocent girl. Continue then. Don't blame me later if I try my luck with him.'

'Nisha, just fuck off.'

Juhi wished she'd said yes to the coffee, but it had been so unexpected. After having her lunch, she went back to her workstation and thought about the moment.

'Abhay Diwan,' Juhi repeated his name in her mind and took out her phone to find him on social media. After scrolling a bit, she found his profile on Facebook as well as Instagram. Unfortunately, his Facebook profile was locked and she couldn't even see him clearly in his display picture.

Luckily, his Instagram profile was public, and as soon as Juhi saw that, she turned off the screen of her phone fearing someone around would notice. After confirming that there was no one about, she opened his profile again. She read his bio which said, *If you are reading my bio, that means you are interested. Then why hesitate to follow?*

Juhi stopped herself from following him but continued to scroll through his pictures. The more she looked at them, the more she felt for him. There were pictures with many friends, even girls, and family. There was one photo of him on the beach, in swimming trunks, which he had posted a couple of weeks ago. He didn't have six-pack abs or a toned body, but he looked very lean and fit. To have a closer look, she zoomed into the picture and her thumb slipped and she accidently liked it.

Fuck! Fuck! What have I done? Will he think I'm a total creep? OMG. Why, why? I just hope he does not have push notifications. Maybe he won't realise if I unlike it right now. Hopefully. But what if he is online? Shit, I am doomed.

Juhi unliked the post right away and kept her fingers crossed. Luckily, when he returned, he didn't react or even notice her. And that actually made her happy for the time being.

Now I am sure God exists. Thank you so much! I will never commit such a mistake again.

Later that night, she had a smile on her face thinking about it. She did stalk him again, but was extra cautious to not like his picture.

Juhi didn't interact with him for the next few days, but she had entered a loop where, every day, she checked him out, stalked him on social media and had sleepless nights thinking about him. It was like Abhay had taken over her mind and had formed a kingdom there. She had casually dived into the pool of love only to realise she couldn't swim.

• •

'I'm leaving a bit early from office today,' Nisha said as they had their lunch.

'Going on a date with the boyfriend or someone else?' Juhi teased.

'Why do you have so much of problem? And anyway, you are soon entering the club of couples. Then we will go together,' Nisha played along.

Juhi rubbished her saying, 'In your dreams. I don't love anyone.'

'Ya, I can see it from the last few days. To be specific, since Abhay joined.'

'Nonsense.'

'You may not admit it, but it's evident in your expressions and gestures. The way you look at him, the way you observe the things he does in the office ...'

Juhi actually checked in the camera of her phone if her expressions revealed her feelings, but she saw nothing different in her face. After lunch, Juhi was alone in the passage returning from the restroom when she saw Abhay walking in her direction. He smiled as he passed by. Juhi smiled back. She decided to wait in the passage next to the water cooler, thinking it was the right time to chat with him.

What will I say? Hi, I am Juhi ... no, he might already know my name. Hi, I'm sorry for liking your picture. No ... what if he hasn't noticed it. Okay, I will just compliment his shirt. Hi Abhay, blue really suits you. Ya, this is fine.

'Hi Abhay, nice shirt—blue really suits you. Hi Abhay, nice shirt—blue really suits you.' She kept rehearsing her lines and when she saw him coming out of the restroom, she quickly filled a glass with water. She just hoped she looked confident. But as he inched closer, she couldn't bring herself to say anything; she only managed to exchange smiles with him again.

I wonder if I will ever gather the courage to talk with him, she thought. She felt disheartened.

Coming back to her seat, she observing him keenly. Blue really did suit him well.

The way you are holding your coffee cup in one hand and talking on the phone is really adorable. Whoever you are talking to with that broad smile will surely have a good day ahead. You have that optimism and spark in you.

Okay, you are back to work. I must say, you are very enthusiastic about work considering you are a new employee. You hardly even look up from your computer. It shows how dedicated you are. Committed.

Whenever you get up from your seat, you give me goose bumps. Now, you wanted to go to the team lead's desk, but I felt you would walk up to me. Doesn't matter. I don't know why I get so nervous around you. I usually feel uncomfortable around boys, and I'm not that outspoken. But with you it's different.

After wrapping up her work for the day, she went to the ATM on the ground floor lobby to withdraw cash. She inserted the debit card and, after collecting the cash, tried to remove the card, but it was stuck. She tried a couple of times, and even pressed the exit button multiple times, but to no avail. That activated her panic mode and she looking around for the security guard, but he wasn't in his place. There were no familiar faces in the lobby, and she was reluctant to take help from an unknown person. She thought of giving it another try, and that's when she felt someone standing behind her. She turned around to see that it was Abhay. Her heart skipped a beat .

Her panic mode was elevated further when Abhay, seeing the expression on her face, calmly asked her , 'Any problem? Can I help?'

She just looked at him for a few seconds and then finally said, 'My card has got stuck. Can you please do something?'

'Let me try. It happened with me once and I managed to remove it.'

Juhi took a step back and gazed at him as he touched her card. He held the exit button for a few seconds and pulled the card outside.

'There it is.'

Juhi felt relieved. She didn't understand whether to curse that ATM machine or thank her fate for putting her in that situation.

'Thanks,' she mumbled.

'You want me to drop you somewhere?'

Juhi shook her head and said, 'No, I am good.'

She was sure that Abhay could sense her unease while talking with him. But she was helpless. She followed him to the parking area where her Scooty was parked. Abhay waved his hand to bid goodbye and rode away when she too raised her hand. Till he went out of her sight, Juhi stood there, unable to believe what had just happened.

She was about to sit on her Scooty when she saw Abhay coming back into the parking premises.

Has he forgotten something inside, she wondered.

He rode up to where she was standing and said, 'I thought of taking you for a coffee ...'

Juhi couldn't say no this time. She had been waiting for this moment. Little had she expected that she would get a chance to sit on his bike. He insisted she go with him and leave the Scooty in the parking lot. They didn't speak much till they reached the café. Once inside, he pulled out a chair for her.

'What would you like to order? If not coffee, this café serves amazing red velvet cake. You must try it.'

Juhi looked up from the menu. Abhay was staring at her so intensely that she was sure he was able to see the smallest flecks of imperfections on her skin.

'Okay, I don't mind,' Juhi said. The rasp in his voice had her craving to hear more from him. She could sense the heat coursing through her cheeks, tinting them a subtle shade of pink. She always felt awkward interacting with guys, though this was new to her—the blush that always seemed to make an appearance when he was around.

'Has anyone told you that you are really beautiful?' Abhay said.

His demeanour showed he was being genuine and she couldn't help but smile. She was aware of her imperfections, but the way Abhay looked at her and the words he spoke made her feel empowered.

As he spoke, she noticed the crinkles by his eyes and the depth in his gaze. He looked adorable in that moment and she wanted nothing more than to snap a picture so she would have a memento.

'You know, the day I saw you in the office, I fell for you. I didn't know how you felt so I didn't do anything, but when I observed that you too were looking at me, I decided to wait for the right time. Today was it.'

Oh no, he caught me observing him all the time. And I thought he didn't have the slightest of clues.

His words brought her back to her senses and she quickly tried to cover up, 'No, I was not eyeing you. I just found you attractive and smart, so you see ... I was not stalking you or anything. I really didn't think that you'd noticed me.'

'Madam ... are you okay?'

A strong light flashed in front of her eyes and everything vanished. She was kicked back into the real word to see she was still standing near her Scooty and the security guard was by her side.

'Madam, are you okay? Is something wrong or are you waiting for someone?'

What the fuck, she thought. She shook her head. 'I am fine. I was just leaving,' she said and left for home.

When she reached, she saw Nisha and Gautam watching a movie.

'Weren't you both supposed to be going out?' Juhi asked, leaving her handbag on the table.

'We thought of just relaxing at home. We had some red velvet cake in a café and returned. By the way, why are you later than usual? Did you also go on a date?'

'Ya, even I had red velvet cake,' Juhi replied, and Nisha laughed.

Juhi went into the kitchen to have some water when she heard Gautam say, 'Juhi … I heard you are in love? Is it true?'

'Don't take your girlfriend seriously,' Juhi retorted from inside and went straight into her bedroom.

Juhi knew that Nisha wasn't wrong. She too felt that she was in love. But would she be able to express it to him was a question to which even she had no answer.

I've never been the type to say what I feel. Basically, I keep everything inside. And with you it is no different. I want to tell you; believe me, I've tried. But there's a part of me that just can't take that chance. So, I doubt that you'll ever know. I guess I'm your secret admirer. That name seems to fit just right.

Three

'Gautam, do you really love Nisha?' Juhi asked as she prepared breakfast like every day. Being a weekend, no one was in a hurry and they had got up later than usual.

'Of course,' Gautam said and changed the channel on the television. 'Why don't they come up with some nice programs? There's never anything good to watch.'

Juhi was seeking answers though, and threw another question at him. 'When did you sense that you were in love with her?' She wanted to know for sure that what she felt for Abhay was love.

'The day I realised I couldn't get her out of my mind. The day when she made me completely forget my ex who broke up with me. And when I realised all my attention was focussed on her.'

'Aww, that's so sweet, baby. I really want to kiss you right now. You can shower such praises even when we are alone sometimes.' Nisha pulled his cheeks and hugged him.

That's how I feel. He is continuously in my thoughts and he has all my attention too, Juhi said to herself.

'And what about you, Nisha?'

'Why are you asking that?' Nisha asked.

Juhi just wanted an answer. 'Tell me, please. I am asking because you still flirt around despite having Gautam in your life.'

Nisha got up from the sofa and walked towards the dining area where Juhi was serving breakfast. 'Darling, I told you—doctors have said flirting is healthy at times.'

'I am serious.' Juhi looked up.

Nisha saw her expression and said, 'Okay, jokes apart. Look, I know my limits and I never cross them. I do flirt but it doesn't go further than that. And most of the time it only makes me realise how special Gautam is. The way he is with me—those idiots with whom I flirt with could never be like that. I would never break his trust.'

I think she is right. Even I never felt anyone was special before Abhay. Juhi now wanted to know how Nisha had sensed that she was in love.

'What made you—'

Before she could complete her sentence, Nisha interrupted. 'Now will you tell me why you are asking such questions in the morning? I feel like we are on some couples dating show.'

Juhi sat down and took a deep breath. 'Okay, I need to tell you guys something.'

'What is it?' Nisha asked curiously. She had somewhat guessed it already.

'The thing is ... I think I love Abhay. When he is around, I can't take my eyes off him. His body language, his clothes, his hair ... okay everything. However, when he's near me, I behave like he doesn't exist. I have tried not to do this, a thousand times, but it just automatically happens. When I see him, I long for him to look at me. I want him to catch my gaze again and again. When he says "hi" but doesn't continue the conversation, I desperately want him to keep talking to me. I make myself seem unapproachable involuntarily, and it makes me hate myself. I still don't know why I react like that. What should I do?'

'Damn, that was a bloody long monologue. Never seen you like this in the past couple of years. I kept telling you to hook up with guys but you were always adamant. And now look at you. You are totally in love,' Nisha stated, patting her friend's back, congratulating her for finally falling in love.

'And that scares me. He barely notices me. I don't know how to make him feel the same way I do.'

'Try to impress him. Look good. Present yourself in a way so that he would not be able to resist you,' Gautam said.

'Don't listen to him. Just be the way you are,' Nisha rubbished him.

Juhi however took Gautam's suggestion seriously; she felt Abhay would never notice her if she stayed the way she was.

Come on Juhi, you have to do it for Abhay, your love. She made up her mind to put some effort into herself.

When Gautam had left, Juhi stood in front of mirror

and asked Nisha, 'Do you think I should change my hairstyle? Will that work?'

'Yes, shave your head completely. He will certainly notice you then. And if he doesn't, then I'll shave his head for sure.'

But Juhi was in no mood to joke. She didn't move away from the mirror. 'How about my eyebrows? I think they are a little thick.'

'Do you think I have done a fucking beauty salon course that I can give you tips about your eyebrows? Stop irritating me. It's just today you have told me that you are in love and I am already getting pissed off by your actions.'

'Okay, get lost,' Juhi reacted angrily.

On Monday, when she reached office, she looked totally different. She had got her hair cut and bought new clothes, making Nisha wonder what next. Though she was wearing formals as usual, the cut was different—she looked more elegant and the colours complemented her wheatish complexion.

Juhi wanted to make sure Abhay noticed, and thus intentionally walked near his desk a couple of times. But she didn't get any reaction. Eventually, she lost hope and continued working.

At lunch time, Abhay came near her desk and said, 'You're looking really nice today.'

Juhi froze for a moment and looked at him like a colour-blind person seeing colour for the first time. She thought he would not notice the change, but he had, and that gave her goose bumps. She wanted to hug him right there and tell him how much she loved him.

It's working, yes, it's working. It was just a compliment and then he walked off, but even that means so much to me. At least he complimented me. His few words are enough to make my day. I think I have to work more on myself now to gain all his attention.

This was followed by her getting conscious about her weight.

No burgers, no pizza, no cheese and no sweets. At least for the next one month till I lose a few kilos. I hate doing this but I have to do it.

She filled up the fridge with green vegetables and fat-free food. Nisha had no clue whatsoever until, just before dinner, Juhi revealed, 'From today, we will only eat salad.'

'Now what's this new drama?' Nisha said.

'We both need to follow a strict healthy diet,' Juhi said, sorting out the vegetables for dinner.

'We? What do you mean by "we"? Why should I diet; I don't need it.'

'You have to. You have also gained weight because of your drinking habits and eating junk,' Juhi said in a convincing tone but Nisha was not falling for it.

'Look, keep me out of it please.'

'No. You too along with me will have green tea every day now.'

'What the fuck. No way. I feel pukish after drinking green tea.'

'What rubbish. Even Priyanka Chopra has it,' Juhi tried to motivate her, but it was of no use.

'She is an actress. And her husband is Nick Jones. My boyfriend is Gautam, who too has a beer belly. When he walks into a room, first his beer belly enters and then the rest of his body.' Nisha laughed.

'You have no option. Otherwise, cook for yourself.'

'This is not done, Juhi. You are creating a rift in our friendship. After following a diet for fifteen days, you will realise that all you have lost are fifteen days. Nothing else,' Nisha said.

But Juhi was firm in her decision and because Nisha didn't want to cook, she too ended up eating salad for dinner. The next morning, when Nisha got up, she saw Juhi exercising in the living room.

'I am going to kill Gautam for feeding you this shit. Because of him even I have to suffer now,' she said.

Juhi just gave her a look and continued with her squats. Nisha went into the kitchen to prepare tea for herself and came out running the next moment.

'Where's the sugar?'

'I hid the box so that we don't give in to temptation. I have kept sugar-free tablets near the microwave,' Juhi replied.

'No ... this is not happening! Are you serious?'

'Yes. Trust me, in a couple of days, you will get used to it.'

'I hope I survive till then.' Nisha sighed. Then she said, 'And what about breakfast?'

'Breakfast is on the table,' Juhi said as she continued her exercises.

Nisha went towards the dining table thinking she would at least have a good breakfast if not morning tea.

But she had to face disappointment again. She pretended to cry like a child who is denied chocolate.

'I am going to throw you out of this house very soon, I think. What is this? Just one boiled egg for breakfast?'

'Not only for breakfast. We are going to have it for lunch too.'

'Holy crap. Why do I have to face this torture? Better I tell Abhay about your feelings. We will get clarity today itself and then we can live a normal life.'

Neither did Juhi take Nisha's comment seriously nor did she change her plan. For the next fifteen days, she followed the diet and even made Nisha do it. Not only this, she also made Nisha do weird chin exercises for her jawline and insisted that they take the stairs to their apartment.

'Juhi, for fifteen days we've been eating this crap. When are we switching back to normal?' Nisha asked, seeing mushroom salad again for the dinner. 'Anyway Abhay is least bothered about what and how you are doing.'

'That's a little mean, don't you think?' Juhi's expression showed hurt and discomfort.

Nisha immediately felt bad about her words.

'But I think you are right,' Juhi said. She put her cutlery away on one side of her plate and leaned back in her chair.

'Juhi, I should not have said it like that. I'm sorry,' Nisha said.

Juhi was upset, not with Nisha, but with herself. Even after putting in so much effort, Abhay hadn't tried to talk to her or pay her any extra attention. There had just been a formal compliment now and then over the past two weeks.

'I don't think this is going to work. I don't know what I should do so that he begins to have feelings for me. I am so tired and have started feeling very negative about everything.'

'Don't be sad. At least you started liking yourself in the process of getting fit. And along with you, even I have lost some weight. See?' Nisha tried to make her smile.

But Juhi was feeling extremely low and went into her bedroom without finishing her dinner. She wanted to call her dad and talk with him but she didn't. Eventually she called her brother and told him what was happening.

'Didi, I feel you should just talk with him. Tell him that you like him and express whatever your heart feels,' Suyash said after hearing her story.

'Are you sure?'

'Of course I am.'

'I am scared to tell him. In fact, I don't have the guts to even talk to him normally. Whenever he says something, I feel like I lose all my confidence to speak.'

'Don't worry. Sometimes even guys are shy to express how they feel. Don't forget to tell me what happens. All the best.'

Juhi thought for a while and decided to confess her feelings to Abhay. She even told Nisha about it.

'Now, that's my girl,' Nisha said.

'You think I can do it?'

'You will. Chill.' Nisha sounded positive. 'Also that means from tomorrow we are eating anything and everything, right?

Juhi laughed at that. But she was nervous from within.

I have to get it off my chest. Holding it in for so long has become unbearable. It feels like something is growing inside of me and it's getting harder day by day; harder to keep it inside and control it. There are only two options now. Either confess or let it go. And I don't want to let him go. I love him. I really do.

Being in love gives you a sense of belonging but gathering the courage to confess that love to someone gives you anxiety. It's like holding a burp in for a long time. You wonder if holding it in will make the feeling go away, but do it for too long and it begins to hurt. She had a similar strong urge. Not to burp, but to confess the feelings to someone she loved with all her heart!

'You really think I have taken the right decision?' she said. 'What if ...'

'If you ask me, you have no choice,' Nisha said. She took a sip of her black coffee and went to stand beside her friend in the balcony of their apartment.

Seeing the anxiety in her eyes, Nisha said, 'Look, I know that falling in love is the most wonderful feeling, but you should also be with that person you love. For that, one of you needs to propose to the other at some point in time.'

Nisha's words comforted her to some extent, yet the turbulence in her head didn't calm down.

She loved him so intensely that she didn't want to lose him. She loved the feeling of being in love with him and didn't want to let it go. That's why she preferred to love him silently.

The next morning she reached office determined to propose to him. She and Nisha entered the lift along with other people, and Juhi's heart melted. There he was! Abhay! He was looking dapper in formals, his face covered with a slight stubble. He entered the lift just before the doors closed, and Nisha quickly stepped out and winked at her. The lift was crowded, but she could see only him.

Act normal, she said to herself. *What should I say? I need to practice my lines before I say anything.* In her mind, she rehearsed what she was going to say. *'Abhay, I wanted to say something … Abhay, I love you.'* She kept repeating the lines over and over again until there were only three of them left in the lift. She checked the floor number the other guy had pressed.

Damn, only we three are left and this guy will get off on the seventh floor, and then it's just us in the lift. Just the thought of it is giving me butterflies.

Her nervousness increased with every floor. If Abhay had turned to look behind, he would have sensed there was something terribly wrong with this girl.

Seventh floor. The lift beeped.

There he goes! It was only the two of them now. Her heart was pounding.

Fourteenth floor. The lift beeped again and she came to reality. She was still standing behind him and as soon as the door opened, he stepped out. She wanted to stop him and tell him how much she loved him, but only gazed after him as he walked into the office.

Nisha had reached the floor in a different lift by now and rushed up to ask, 'What happened? Did you tell him?'

'No, I didn't, I can't. Not today at least.' She started walking towards the office entrance.

'Damn, what's wrong with you?' Nisha said, frustrated.

'Nothing. Today isn't the right day.'

'All of sudden you got this realisation, right?

'Ya, I checked the horoscope for today and it says my love life is complicated and I should not take any major decisions today.'

'Wow, looks like you are never going to talk to him in this lifetime. If you leave it up to these two-rupee horoscope guys, you will stay atmanirbhar for the rest of your life.'

'Whatever,' she said, and walked into the office.

• •

Juhi was disappointed with herself. She blamed herself for not being able to open up. She was aloof whenever she chatted with him in the office even though she yearned to know more about him. The more she got acquainted with him, the more she was sure that she loved him. But how could she break out of this cage she had built around herself?

Suddenly, she got an idea. What if she could talk to him as someone else? She could use Nisha's LinkedIn ID. Nisha rarely used it and her login credentials were saved on Juhi's laptop when she had used it once. Juhi was sure

Nisha would not find out, and even if she did, she would not have any problem. So when she got home from office, when Nisha was out with Gautam, she sent Abhay a request. She didn't know if Abhay used that ID or not, but decided to try her luck.

Every few minutes she checked if he had accepted it, and finally, a few hours later, she saw that he had. She took a deep breath and felt like announcing it to the world. In that moment, she completely forgot that Abhay had accepted Nisha's request, not hers. She was just happy that she could finally interact with him the way she wanted. She wondered how to start a conversation, finally deciding on a casual greeting.

'Hi, what's up. What's going on?'

'Nothing much, but why chatting on LinkedIn?' Abhay replied.

Juhi thought a bit and replied, 'I just saw your profile in my recommendations and thought of adding you.'

'Oh, okay.'

Damn, this is heading nowhere. What should I text for the conversation to continue? I'll ask him indirectly. Anyway, my identity is hidden, Juhi said to herself. She messaged, 'Are you liking the vibe of the company? What about the "friendly" girls you mentioned?'

Juhi eagerly waited for his reply.

'Are you asking about yourself?' he texted back.

'Me and Juhi both.'

'Juhi? Why are you asking about her? Something fishy?'

Oh no! Is he suspicious? I think I should slow down.

'Nothing. Just like that.' Juhi tried to cover up.

For almost a minute Abhay didn't respond and she was nervous that he sensed it wasn't Nisha. She thought of sending a question mark but resisted—that would look odd.

Abhay replied after some time, 'Sorry, had to attend a call. Anyway, I have to get back to something. Talk to you later on WhatsApp. See ya.'

WhatsApp? Does Nisha have Abhay's number? She never told me. And if that's the case, then I am gone. What if he tells her? Shit, I have to ask her when she comes back in the night.

Nisha got home at around midnight and Juhi asked her the moment she entered the apartment, 'Nisha, do you have Abhay's number?'

'Yes. Why what happened?' Nisha said. She was a little tipsy.

'You never told me,' Juhi said, upset.

'What's the big deal?' Nisha said as she took off her shoes and lay down on the sofa. She was clearly tired, but kept her eyes open to reply to Juhi's questions.

'I have something to tell you.' Juhi sat beside her.

'Why are you sounding so strange? Even Abhay was sending me weird messages. What's wrong with everyone?' she said, and crashed out the next moment.

Juhi had her heart in her mouth when she heard that. She took Nisha's phone from her handbag and opened her WhatsApp. There were messages from Gautam, her family and other friends but Juhi was interested in only one name. Abhay. She opened the chat and saw that messages had been exchanged an hour before. Her hands trembled as she started reading.

Abhay: Hi, let's talk here. I am not very active on LinkedIn. Luckily had logged in today to update my work profile when I saw your request.

Nisha: My request? Not sure what you're talking about. I'm in a club having drinks with my boyfriend. And I'm sure I am not that drunk to open LinkedIn from here. :D

Abhay: Are you sure?

Nisha: Of course. Yes, I have had a few drinks more than usual but still. :p

Abhay: Does anyone apart from you use your LinkedIn?

Nisha: No … but I think Juhi has my password. Maybe it was her. Chill.

Gone, finished, over!

She was furious with Nisha for revealing it to him, no matter how drunk she was. What would Abhay's reaction be? The question haunted her the whole night. If 'I am screwed badly' had a face, it would have looked similar to Juhi's expression at that moment. She had fucked up, and how!

Four

Nisha got up the next morning with a terrible headache. She put her hands on her head and grunted in pain. She looked for Disprin tablets, which she generally kept in the bedside drawer. After having one, she looked for her phone. She had blurred memories of what had happened last night and had no idea of the storm coming her way. It was only when she opened her WhatsApp chat that she realised her blunder. She instantly got out of her bed as she read Abhay's chats and went outside her room to see Juhi pouring tea into her cup. Hoping for some sympathy from Juhi, she held her head as if she was in pain and unwell.

Juhi didn't show any concern and brought up the topic the next minute.

'I am sure you have checked your phone and realised what happened yesterday,' she said.

'Juhi, I have no idea when I chatted with him! I should have asked you first before saying anything to him,' Nisha said with a gloomy face.

Juhi didn't even look at her as she poured tea in Nisha's cup too. She said, 'I don't know how I'm going to face him now! What will he think about me?'

'We'll sort it out. I'll tell him that it wasn't you but me who texted him.'

Juhi shook her head. She knew what Nisha was saying made no sense. 'I don't think we can mend it now. I was stupid for thinking I should interact with him as you. I shouldn't have used your LinkedIn. Let's see how he reacts, that's all we can do and hope it doesn't end in a terrible way.'

Nisha didn't say anything. She quietly ate her breakfast as Juhi tried to think of ways to defend what she had done. She didn't even feel like eating, but forced herself to take a few bites of her cereal before putting it aside. She got up from her seat to get ready when her phone beeped. It was a WhatsApp message from an unknown number. She read the name mentioned in the message and hurriedly opened it. It was Abhay.

'Hi, good morning. Abhay this side. Wanted to message you last night itself but was not sure if you were awake.'

Juhi stood still, shocked. She checked the display picture to confirm it was really him. She re-read the message again, unsure what she should say. She tried to figure out what exactly he wanted to message, reading the text with different inflections. Who had given her number to him?

'It's Abhay,' she said, shock still clear in her voice.

Nisha gulped down the entire bite in her mouth hearing that and, noticing the way Juhi was looking at her, said, 'Now don't give me that look. I didn't give him your number. Someone else from office must have.'

'What should I say?' Juhi was totally blank.

'Chat casually. Don't bring up the topic until he says something,' Nisha suggested and walked to her side.

Juhi's heart was racing. She typed, 'Hey, good morning. I was awake. What's up? On the way to office?'

Abhay replied instantly.

'Leaving in sometime. By the way, sorry to message you randomly. I got your number from Arpit. Hope you don't mind.'

Juhi decided not to follow Nisha's suggestion and said, 'Look, I know I goofed up yesterday and am really embarrassed about it. Nisha had asked me to check some updates and I forgot that I was logged in from her account and not mine. Your profile appeared in recommendations,' Juhi said.

Nisha was peering into her phone as curious as Juhi, as they waited for his reply.

'You should thank my whiskey for getting a message from Abhay,' Nisha said.

'Shut up. Why hasn't he replied?'

'You should take some dating tips from me. I won't even charge you. The way he texted first, I'm sure it's all good,' Nisha said.

She was right. Juhi received a reply.

'Don't be embarrassed. It's totally fine. I was just confused—instead of talking directly, why you would do this.'

Juhi felt relieved and without hesitating replied, 'Thank God. You seriously didn't feel bad, right?'

'No, not at all. Why would I? After all, as you said, I have the company of friendly girls.'

'Ya, ya ... absolutely.' She sent this along with a star-struck emoji.

'Okay, see you in office.'

'Sure. See ya.'

Juhi looked at Nisha who was giving her a teasing look. She said, 'Now I take back my crappy sorry and I want you to fucking thank me.'

Juhi, with a big smile on her face, hugged her. She couldn't believe what had just happened.

'See, in such matters, drinking helps. If you would have had a drink on the very first day you saw Abhay, you would have been in his arms and not mine, kissing him, cuddling him and what not.'

'Please ...'

The intoxicating feeling rejuvenated her. All those hours waiting to talk to him, all the sessions in her head wondering what was going on in his mind and what she should say that wouldn't create a bad impression, the constant checking in the mirror—all of it had led to this most unforgettable moment.

When she reached office, Abhay was already there and, seeing her, he walked towards her and said, 'You seem to be in peppy mood today, looking at your smile. And, of course, you look beautiful as usual.'

Juhi blushed hearing that and said, 'Thanks, but again, I just wanted to say I'm really sorry for yesterday.' A nervous smile escaped her lips when she made direct eye contact with him.

Abhay smiled at her. 'I told you to relax. It's fine.'

Juhi looked into his eyes and then turned away. She could stare at him all day, but she didn't want to give her feelings away. Her eyes were a window to her soul and if she had stared a little more, she knew that she wouldn't be able to hide her love.

Noticing the awkward silence, Nisha said, 'That's what I told her. She is unnecessarily over-reacting.'

Abhay was amused, she could see. The subtle manner in which his lips turned up into a smile would have been easy to miss if her eyes hasn't been on him just before. He folded his arms, and said, looking at both the girls, 'So how about having our pending coffee today in the evening? I hope you have no problem today at least.'

Nisha thought it was time for Juhi to break the ice. She said, 'I'm sure Juhi doesn't have a problem. But I have a date with my boyfriend. You guys carry on though, I don't mind.'

'Works for me. Are you up for it?' Abhay asked, his eyes locked on Juhi.

'Sure, I don't mind,' Juhi replied. She couldn't have asked for anything more. She didn't know if it was the previous day's episode that had made him open up or the efforts she had taken over the last few weeks. Whatever it was, it seemed everything was going right for her.

You might think I am silly or immature after yesterday's act; I know you are not revealing it to me, but you are not wrong. You can say that I am a little immature in matters of dating, but now that you are with me, I will overcome that too. I have dreamt about going on a date with you several times, but it's happening for real today and you don't know how much exhilaration just the thought of it brings to my heart.

Juhi couldn't wait for evening to come. It was a hectic day for her, but post lunch, when she got some buffer time, Nisha put forth a suggestion. 'I feel you should tell him today that you love him. If you feel it's the moment, just go for it. Don't hesitate. I can sense that even he has feelings for you.'

'Have you lost it? You want me to tell him in the first meeting itself? It's not a passing fling, I am serious,' Juhi whispered, making sure no one was overhearing their conversation.

'So, what—do you want to play a test match where you have to get used to the conditions and then play your shots? At least throw some hints at him so that you can figure out what is going on in his mind.'

'I'll see. I don't want to rush and spoil everything,' Juhi said.

As the clock struck six-thirty, she switched off her system. Nisha had left early on purpose. Abhay indicated to Juhi that he needed a few minutes more to complete his work and asked her to wait. Juhi waited in the lobby downstairs. Her heart was beating like a drum; she kept looking towards the elevator every few seconds.

I am already fantasizing about the moment. Will you hold my hand? Will you take me on a dream ride? How's it going to be? Will you make it memorable for me? I can't believe how involved I am already. I never thought a day would come when my happiness would depend on some other person. You have taken over my heart, mind and soul.

'Shall we leave?' All of a sudden, she heard Abhay's voice.

'Ya,' Juhi replied.

They walked towards the main entrance and, seeing Juhi quiet, Abhay asked, 'You are fine, right? I mean, I hope you didn't have any other plans.'

Does he want to know whether I have a boyfriend? How should I tell him that I am already going on a date with my to-be boyfriend!

'No, I don't have any plans. I am just a little tired after such a hectic day. I had to submit at least twenty reports and reply to so many mails.'

'Then I have an idea, something to make your tiredness disappear.'

'What's that?'

'Have you ever tried mastani?'

'Only once, and it wasn't that great.'

'Then done. Instead of going to Barista, there's a Puneri Mastani House about a kilometre away. We can walk there and, trust me, once you have had the mastani there, you will feel refreshed.'

'Okay, if you say so,' Juhi said. Anyway, the place didn't matter to her, or what they were having. Only he did.

The walk to the café seemed more romantic to her than any Bollywood song. They talked casually and she had never felt so at ease with someone before. It made her question all the people she had crossed paths with and also made her regret that she hadn't tried to talk to him earlier. Once they reached the café, Abhay ordered two glasses of mango mastani.

'When did you shift to Pune?' he asked, as they waited for their milkshakes to come. 'Did you complete your graduation here?'

'No, I only came here a couple of years back,' she replied.

'Hope you are loving my Pune,' he said with a smile.

Juhi nodded.

'You seem to be a rather quiet one,' Abhay stated.

'Yeah.'

'Why is that?'

'I don't know. It's just the way I am,' she said.

Just then, the mastanis were served.

'That looks delicious,' Juhi said, looking at the glass in front of her. The extra calories would be worth it, she was sure.

Abhay finished half his mastani in one go and asked Juhi too to have it the same way. She did so and had an urge to burp but controlled it somehow.

'That tasted amazing. You were right,' Juhi said.

Their conversation flowed naturally, and Juhi found that she was truly enjoying his company. She laughed at the ridiculous jokes and stories he narrated. She learnt that he lived with his parents and was their only child, that he had completed his graduation in Pune, and how he got an offer from this company.

I think he likes me too. Otherwise why would he tell me all the details about his life? He wants me to know him well, Juhi thought.

As she was telling him about her hometown, he interrupted. 'You've got something on your lip,' Abhay said with a grin.

'So now that I've decided to talk, you interrupt me?' she teased.

He laughed. 'Let me help you,' he said, getting up from his chair.

'Are we taking the cliché route here?' she said as she wiped her mouth.

Abhay's phone rang then. He turned it on silent, and a minute later, it rang again.

'If it's urgent, take the call,' Juhi said.

'No, it's fine,' Abhay said and ignored the call. But the phone beeped again and he excused himself. 'Give me a moment.'

He got up from his chair and walked away from the table. Juhi could tell that he was arguing with someone.

Who is it on the phone that he had to walk away from me to talk? From his gestures, it looks like he is convincing someone about something. And then the odd awkward smile he is giving me in between is making me doubt whether he already has someone special in his life. No, but why would he come on a date with me then? Now it's been more than ten minutes and he has still not disconnected the call. Is that person more important than me?

Juhi's mind was occupied with thoughts until Abhay came back and took his seat again.

'Sorry. Ya, you were saying something,' Abhay said, placing his phone back on the table.

Juhi was curious to know whose call it was and so she casually asked, 'Was it urgent? I hope everything's fine.'

'Oh ya, that was my girlfriend, Stuti. She's a bit possessive about me and was going berserk for not telling her that I was going out with a colleague. She wants me to do things her way, and I find that cute. I guess all girlfriends are like that,' he said.

Juhi, shell-shocked, didn't respond.

Abhay continued. 'But she is sweet. If I say no to her or don't fulfil her wish, she gets upset with me. And whenever I agree to her point, she's all lovey-dovey. We've been dating each other for a little more than a year now, so we know each other well.'

Juhi felt shaken. *You told me everything about yourself, but you never said that you have a girlfriend. I was beginning to think we shared the same feelings, but I was so wrong. Why didn't you mention her before? I must have seen her in your Instagram pictures, but there was nothing in any of the captions to indicate that she is your girlfriend. I would have not come this far in the hope of your love. My love is yours but now I know your love is not mine.*

Even the thought of him holding somebody else's hand broke her heart. No matter how strong her feelings were for him, the fact was that he loved someone else.

Five

What will you do if the person you love doesn't love you back? Would you surrender anything and everything just to prove your love for him? Would you at least give it a try in order not to have any regrets later? But then what if the person you love loves someone else? Would you still give it a try, overlooking morals and dignity. Or would you just let it go? Whatever you choose, you will be hurt. I can see that now. So, I am not going to let it go. Rather, I can't let it go.

After they left the café and collected their bikes, she followed Abhay, keeping some distance between them. They crossed Hinjewadi and reached Aundh, and then Juhi saw him stop at a corner and get down from his bike. Her heart was trying to convince her mind to leave as she was sure that what she would see now would only hurt her more, but she decided to wait. She was curious to know what his girlfriend looked like, and after a while, Juhi saw someone walking up to Abhay. It was dark, but Juhi could still see her clearly under the streetlight.

On the other side, Abhay had already decided to meet Stuti after she called because she was so angry with him.

Although Stuti loved Abhay wholeheartedly, she was possessive and had a dominating nature that overpowered Abhay's soft personality. Abhay loved that side of her too, however. Neither did he try to supress it nor did he argue with her over it.

The moment Stuti met Abhay, she said, 'Why didn't you tell me that you are going out with someone and that too a girl?'

Abhay smiled and asked her, 'Are you getting jealous?'

'Stop it. I am serious.' Stuti's forehead furrowed with annoyance.

Abhay held her hand lovingly and intertwined his fingers with hers. He brought her close, unconcerned about the people around. He tried to pacify her by kissing her hand and clarified, 'Look, it didn't mean anything. We colleagues had planned to go out for a coffee but one of them had some other plans, and as I was the one to ask them out, it would have looked bad if I had then cancelled. So, Juhi and I went for a coffee. There was nothing more to it.'

Stuti's annoyed expression didn't change. 'Whatever it is. You know I don't like you going out without informing me. If there was nothing in your mind, then why did you have to keep it secret? This is not the first time.'

'Secret? You are taking it to the next level. Anyway, you had told me that you have to work till late, so I thought I wouldn't disturb you.' Abhay pulled her cheeks and added, 'You look cute when you are angry. I love you.'

'Next time, I am not going to listen to such reasons,' Stuti said firmly.

'It's been more than a year now. You should stop being so possessive and doubting me.'

'That's how I am. Didn't you know it from the beginning?' Stuti said.

'Do you know you look too sexy when you show that authority? And then I can't resist holding you tight. I feel like just staring at your lips.' Abhay held her waist and pulled her closer.

'What are you doing? We are on the street.' Stuti could feel his breath as she hugged him. She looked sideways to see if anyone was checking them out. Abhay knew exactly how to calm her down and he did the same.

Their lips brushed against each other for a split second but Stuti pushed him back and said, 'Not now.'

Abhay made her sit on the bike and wore his helmet. Juhi was watching the entire act with a heavy heart. Her eyes became moist seeing Abhay kiss another girl.

I feel horrible. You will never know how I am feeling right now, Abhay. This feeling when you think you've found someone, someone you could truly love with all your heart, but the person loves another. It's devastating. You have your love beside you, Abhay. What about me? I feel my life is sinking and I still hope that you will rescue me.

Juhi reached home and, seeing that Nisha was not in her bedroom, she texted her, 'I hope you have the keys with you.'

She changed into her tracksuit and lay on her bed thinking about how her expectations were shattered. She began sobbing like a child. She rechecked his Instagram and looked at their pictures again. She tried to detach from her feelings but couldn't. Finally, exhausted, she fell asleep.

Meanwhile, Abhay and Stuti had reached her apartment. She had a good salary package which made it possible for her to stay alone in the heart of Pune. Once they had freshened up, Abhay leaned forward, took her face between his hands and kissed her lips. She reciprocated with the same intensity, their lips moulding against each other's perfectly, like pieces of a puzzle fitting together. She leaned closer into him. He dipped down to her neck, his touches showing how crazy she made him.

'Stuti,' he breathed out heavily.

The room was getting unbearably hot, but they didn't care. She fumbled with the edge of the t-shirt she had changed into and pulled it over her head with Abhay's help. She put her arms over his shoulders, noticing the perspiration that had collected on his forehead. She pushed herself closer against him, unintentionally grinding against him. He whimpered as his grip shifted and tightened around her hips. The small space was filled with ragged breaths and sweaty bodies. The room reeked of pheromones and she knew he had reached his peak.

'Did you enjoy it?' Abhay asked her, smiling. However, it was as if his mind wasn't completely there.

'What are you thinking about?' Stuti asked curiously.

Abhay rubbed his eyes. A satisfied sigh filled the air before he pecked her lips tenderly.

'You. My mind is all about you right now.'

Stuti cuddled with him, suddenly tired after the heavy emotional feelings had been stilled. They fell asleep in each other's arms.

Juhi woke up with a shock in her bedroom. Her eyes snapped open, the memory of her dream still vivid. More of a nightmare actually. Her top was drenched in sweat. She removed the blanket and sat upright, staring at the wall. She checked the time—it was barely ten o'clock. She felt lonely, and that emptiness was killing her. The truth had hit her so hard that it was burning her soul. She picked up her phone and called her dad just to hear his voice. She wanted to talk to someone who loved her and valued her presence.

'Papa, I miss you,' she said when her father answered the call, her voice quavering.

'What happened, beta? Are you all right?'

'I'll be fine. But I really miss you guys. I wish I could come there right now.' Juhi wiped her tears and tried to control them. She knew if her dad figured out how upset she was, he would be very worried and she didn't want to trouble them.

'Where's Nisha? You seem upset. Let me talk to her,' her dad asked, concerned.

'She's out with friends. Don't worry, I just called because I am feeling lonely here. I miss the days when we used to sit together and eat, when Maa would oil my hair and whenever I felt sad, you would sit beside me and tell me how important I am to you.'

'Beta, you will always be important to us. You don't need to feel lonely. Nisha's there with you, and if you need, we can come there. And if you feel that you are not content there in Pune, you can come back without any hesitation.'

'Thanks, Papa. I will call you later,' Juhi said and hung up.

She felt better after hearing his voice. Even though she had everyone, she felt alone because everyone was not her only one!

• •

She dreaded going to office the next day. She knew that seeing Abhay would evoke all her emotions. She was also very confused. One minute she felt she should give up, and the next she needed to at least tell him how she felt.

Abhay greeted her in a friendly manner when he reached office, and Juhi tried to respond normally, but Abhay noticed something was wrong.

'Not having a good day?' he asked.

Juhi felt like she had a volcano inside her waiting to erupt and hoped it wasn't showing on her face. 'Nothing, just not feeling good,' she said.

'You'll be fine once the celebration starts in the evening,' Abhay said with a reassuring smile. 'You're coming to the party, right?'

Juhi was confused but nodded her head anyway. When he had left, she turned to Nisha and asked, 'What party?'

'Karan and the other team leaders have organised a party as we cracked the deal and got a new project. He told me some time back and asked me to tell you too,' Nisha revealed.

Juhi sighed. 'I don't want to come. I am not at all in the mood to be around lots of people.'

Nisha turned her chair away from her system towards Juhi. 'You don't need to show that you are dejected because you found out he has a girlfriend.' Juhi had told her everything over breakfast. 'I know you are upset, but don't let him control your emotions. Also, you can't just give up. Yesterday you told me that you would tell him how you feel about him. He doesn't even know that you love him. What do you expect from him in such a situation?'

'Ya, as if we are the leading pair in some Karan Johar movie where in the end everything is fine, and if it isn't, then it's not the end, right?'

Juhi tried hard to concentrate on her work, but every now and then her eyes would move to where he was. Whenever she saw him talking on phone, she felt it was Stuti on the other end and that annoyed her further.

Abhay, completely unaware of Juhi's behaviour, continued his work and, during the lunch break, he called Stuti.

'What's happening, my love?' he asked as he walked towards the cafeteria.

Juhi saw him talking on the phone and said to herself, *I know it's her. You are so lost in her world that you didn't even smile at me when you walked by my desk. I am right here, but sadly my presence is unimportant in your life.*

Stuti replied in a low-spirited voice, 'Working on a PPT. Have a conference in an hour and I am not done yet.'

'Oh, am I disturbing the regional manager who is working really hard?' Abhay teased as he ordered a dosa for himself.

'No, it's fine, tell me. What about you?'

He moved aside from the counter and said, 'I called to tell you that we have an office party in the evening, so we can't meet today.'

'Skip it,' Stuti suggested abruptly.

'I can't. I've just joined the company, it won't give a good impression. I need to gel with everyone.'

'Don't give me all that. It's crap,' Stuti said dismissively.

'What, I am serious.' Abhay took his plate and looked around for a place to sit. He asked her to hold on for a second and connected his ear phones. 'Ya, say.'

'Fine, then I will come to where you guys will be. Anyway your company won't have booked the entire place, like mine does. It will still be open for outsiders.'

Abhay felt a little bad about the way she was putting down his workplace and bragging about hers. But he didn't want to make a fuss. He replied, 'Oh, come on. That would be embarrassing.'

'Now I embarrass you?'

'No, I mean no one's girlfriends or boyfriends are tagging along. It won't look good. You are a professional too, you know how it is.'

'Yours isn't an MNC like mine where you have to follow certain etiquette. It's a side unit of the main firm.'

'Are we trying to prove who's company is superior here?'

'No. So just give in and let me join.'

'Okay, bye.' Abhay disconnected the call, upset by her words.

After eating his lunch, he messaged her, knowing she had an important conference. *'Don't spoil your mood. All the best for the conference. Love you.'*

Stuti didn't reply, but Abhay couldn't hold on to his anger for long. He texted her about the venue and informed Karan about it to avoid an awkward situation.

After they wrapped up work, the entire team headed to Rud Lounge, which was near the office. Karan made a short speech, congratulating everyone on their hard work, and then invited them to head to the floor to dance. Juhi and Nisha were seated with a few others, chatting, but her eyes kept following Abhay wherever he went. He was moving around, talking with a lot of people, a glass of beer in his hand. Soon, he walked over to Juhi and Nisha.

'What are you girls drinking?' he asked, sitting beside Juhi

'I'm drinking whiskey, and she's having a mocktail,' Nisha replied, indicating the glasses in front of them.

'You don't drink alcohol?' Abhay asked Juhi.

'No, I prefer this,' she said, taking a sip of her drink.

Abhay turned towards Nisha. 'You know that you missed mind-blowing mastani yesterday, right?'

Nisha smiled at him. 'Next time for sure.'

Abhay leaned forward to say something more, as the music was loud, when he felt a hand on his shoulder. 'Abhay.' It was Stuti.

Juhi turned and was stunned to see Stuti right behind her. She hadn't expected this at all.

Abhay got up and hugged Stuti tightly. He then made her sit and introduced her to everyone at the table. Stuti shook hands with Juhi, though Juhi's reluctance was clearly visible.

'So, you are the one who had a mastani yesterday. I hope you liked it?' Stuti asked, having a sip of beer from the pint she had ordered.

Juhi smirked and said, 'Yes, and the company too.'

They exchanged a cold look before Abhay, quite oblivious, asked Stuti to come with him to meet Karan.

Juhi watched them walk away, hand in hand.

What girl have you chosen Abhay? She's a creep. You have fallen for the wrong girl. Trust me. Or maybe that's your taste. You deserve better. I could be that girl. I wouldn't be so controlling. I would let you live your life. But will you give me a chance to prove my love?

After some time, Nisha noticed Stuti was standing alone by the bar counter. She looked around for Abhay, and seeing he was busy with Karan, she went up and stood beside Stuti, who was texting someone.

'So, how come you are here?' Nisha asked.

Stuti kept her phone inside and looked up, an annoyed look on her face. 'What does that mean? Abhay is here and I am his girlfriend.'

'I think you took my words the wrong way. Anyway, it's good to meet you.' Nisha smiled at her and, after taking another drink from the counter, went back to her seat.

'Why were you talking with her?' Juhi asked.

'To get some insights.'

'Insights?'

'Darling, I am telling you this girl is here just to check on Abhay. She got annoyed when I asked her about it.'

'How do you know?'

'Experience. There's no other motive to be here. And I am going to take advantage of her insecurity. Just do as I say when I wave at you.' Nisha told her what she had in mind.

After an hour or so, when almost everyone was on the dance floor, Nisha saw Abhay dancing and sensed he was a bit high. She felt it was the right time. She stepped on the dance floor and began to sway to the rhythm of the music. Abhay noticed her and came to where she was dancing. She asked Abhay to dance with her, and he readily agreed. He grabbed her hand and they both swirled around together. Nisha was purposely moving sensually knowing Stuti was watching them. Meanwhile, Juhi went up to Stuti, who was seated at a table nearby. Juhi took the chair adjacent to her and observed the irritation on her face as she watched Nisha and Abhay dance. Her reaction pleased Juhi, and she wanted to irk her more.

'Was Abhay always like this?' she asked.

Stuti looked at Juhi and raised her eyebrows

questioningly. Juhi added, 'I mean, he flirts with everyone in the office. Was he always this flirtatious?'

Stuti didn't react. She was already furious seeing Abhay dancing with a girl and even touching her in a half-drunk state. No doubt, the touch was only part of the dance moves, but Stuti wasn't taking it casually. Stuti had a list of dos and don'ts for Abhay, and this act of his was certainly in the don'ts. Probably topped the list. She got up in a rage and walked towards Abhay. Abhay was so involved in dancing, he didn't realise Stuti was standing behind him. When he did see her, he said, 'Hey baby, I hope you're enjoying yourself.'

'Not really, but you seem to having a great time. You continue, I am leaving,' she said and walked away.

Abhay left the dance floor immediately and followed her.

'Why are you making a scene here? That's the reason I didn't want you to come.'

'Right, so that you can dance with girls and touch them wherever you want.'

'What nonsense.'

'I am done with you, Abhay. We had an argument yesterday itself and today you are again repeating your behaviour in a different way. I think I deserve better than you for sure.'

Abhay tried to stop her but Stuti left.

'See, I told you, experience matters.' Nisha patted her own back.

'*Jahapana tussi great ho* ...' Juhi saluted her and they both had a laugh.

Abhay tried to call Stuti several times but she didn't pick up. He was not really in his senses and, in the wrath of the moment, he sent her a WhatsApp message. 'That was really ridiculous behaviour from your side. I wasn't fucking around that you had to get so agitated. Every time I keep my mouth shut when you talk rubbish about me and my career. But you just always want to prove that you are better than me. That's not how a relationship works. It's about complementing each other, not competing with each other. If you deserve better, then please fuck off. Even I don't want to be with a person who can't let me live freely. Bye, be happy!'

• •

Over the next couple of days, Juhi could see that Abhay was upset. She guessed that they had not been able to sort things out after their fight.

I feel she doesn't value you and, Abhay, you shouldn't be with someone who doesn't care if you are hurt. If I had been in her place, I would have sorted it out the next moment. No ... wait, I wouldn't have let the situation arise. I will make you realise that I am the only one who can love you that way. No one else.

After office that day, Abhay was waiting at the elevator door, lost in thought. Juhi approached him and said, 'You look disturbed, what's the matter? Is Stuti still upset with you?'

'We are not together anymore. She broke up with me.'

Juhi didn't know whether she should jump with joy or show empathy. But looking at the dark circles under his eyes and his distressed face, she felt bad. 'I am so sorry. Didn't mean to hurt you.'

'No ... the one who shouldn't have has already left me hurt.' They stepped into the elevator.

I know you want to be left alone, but I want to cheer you up and bring back that alluring smile of yours that captured my heart.

'I have an idea!' Juhi snapped her fingers.

'What's that?' Abhay asked dully.

Juhi had a sparkle in her eyes. 'Remember last time I was feeling low and what you had proposed?'

Abhay didn't need a second to think. He answered, 'Mastani.' He gave a small smile.

'That's right. So, let's have one. And you'll feel good.'

'No, not now,' Abhay said, getting out of the elevator.

'Oh, come on. I'll pay, you don't need to worry about it,' Juhi teased as she looked into his eyes. 'Don't think. Let's just go.'

Abhay felt bad to say no to her, knowing that she was only trying to cheer him up again.

At the restaurant, Juhi ordered the mastani, placed her hands on the table and looked at him. He felt better seeing the sympathy on her face; it felt like there was at least someone who cared.

'Thanks. For this treat. I really needed this.'

Juhi's smiled. 'I know, and that's why I didn't want to leave you alone. I understand how it feels.'

'You have gone through this?' Abhay asked curiously.

Juhi shook her head. 'No, but I have seen others.'

After a brief silence, Abhay said, 'You know, whenever we fight, it's always me who takes the initiative to sort things out. She is always too proud to take that step. Sometimes I feel so inferior when she boasts about her achievements and dismisses what I have done. I never stop her from doing what she wants. Be it hanging out with friends or pursuing her dreams. It's always me who has taken a back-step for her growth; I have always given her preference over my job and career and now she makes me regret it.'

Juhi could hear the grief in his voice.

'Can I tell you something?' she asked hesitantly.

'Sure.' Abhay moved forward, resting his elbows on the table.

'Don't feel bad, but I think that Stuti isn't the right girl for you. It seems she really controls your entire life. You deserve better.'

Abhay remained silent. Stuti's words—that she deserved better than him—came back to him.

Their mastanis arrived at that moment and he had his in one go. It did feel as if it lightened his mood. He reached out and held Juhi's hand, and his touch increased her heartbeat. He said, 'I like your company. Thanks for being there.'

'I'll always be there.' Juhi tightened her grip on his hand.

I know you'll love me one day. At least now you feel better in my company. And I promise, you won't feel this relationship is toxic! I know now it's just a matter of time and we will be together forever. I love you!

• •

The next few weeks, Juhi and Abhay spent most of their time together, both in and out of office. Juhi couldn't have asked for more. She was elated. She had never felt this comfortable with anyone.

Abhay and Stuti were still not on talking terms and no messages had been exchanged. But Abhay couldn't stop thinking about her. He was adamant that he would not be the one to initiate a reconciliation, though. To avoid more depressing thoughts, he asked Juhi if she would like to see a movie.

She was getting ready, when Nisha asked her, 'Going out with Abhay?'

'Yes, we are going for a movie at PVR,' Juhi replied, adjusting the straps of her dress.

'Movie and all. That's something. You know why guys like to watch movies, right?' Nisha asked. She sat down on the bed and watched Juhi do her make-up.

'I am sure you have a theory behind it and you won't get relief till you speak it out.'

'You know me well.' Nisha beamed. 'It's because they want to get cosy with you. So, don't shy away from a kiss. And if things go well, you never know.'

'Can't you think straight ever?'

'I am serious. You'll soon see it for yourself,' Nisha said, putting on a serious look.

'Okay bye. I am leaving. And if you are right, then please don't disturb us by texting. You could spoil the moment,' Juhi played along, laughing.

They were supposed to meet directly at the mall, so she got into a cab and texted him that she was on the way. She wondered what was waiting for her.

I don't know what's going on in your mind. Are we going to kiss today? Honestly, I am fine with it, but is that the only thing on your mind? If so, then it's not something I am looking for. I want your love, true love. From what I know of you, you are not someone who randomly hooks up with girls. You are genuine, honest and sweet. That's why I love you. In fact, today I am going to propose to you. I feel it's the right time to take things ahead.

Abhay was waiting by the entrance of the mall. She walked up to him and he said, 'You are looking gorgeous in this white dress. I am sure you will turn many heads today.'

Juhi blushed and didn't say anything.

'Shall we go inside?' Abhay asked.

Juhi nodded and they went into the theatre. The movie started and different thoughts ran in Juhi's mind.

Will he, won't he? Will he, won't he?

But Abhay didn't. The movie got over and they stepped outside. Juhi was relieved.

So, Nisha was wrong this time. You didn't make the first move. But I wanted her to be wrong. I wanted to see if you love me truly or if it's just lust. You proved me right. You love me. Then let's express it.

They went to the food court and ordered from McDonald's.

'I loved the climax of the movie. I thought it would be a sad ending, but the way the story twisted was fantastic.'

'I know. The last scene brought tears to my eyes,' Juhi said.

After they'd finished eating, Juhi thought this was the moment. She gazed at him; his eyes were locked on hers too. It was like everyone around had blurred and it was just the two of them sitting there. Juhi broke the silence.

'I have a gift for you.'

'A gift? Wow. What is it?'

She placed her bag on the table between them and pulled out the gift she had got.

'Here it is,' she said, handing it over to him.

Like a kid, Abhay immediately unwrapped it. It was a special edition watch and Abhay's eyes widened when he saw it.

'Why this, though?'

'I wanted to tell you this since a long time ... But I don't know where to start. I never thought I'd be saying this, but the last few weeks have been the best in my life, and I want the days ahead of me to be great too.'

'What do you mean?' Abhay couldn't understand what she was trying to say.

Juhi took a deep breath and said, 'I love you. I really do. I can't imagine that I would be nearly as happy if I didn't have you in my life. I lose my sense of time when I am around you. I want to be with you. Forever.'

Abhay was stunned to hear her revelation. He reached out and held her hand. Juhi trembled as she wondered what he would say. After a minute, he replied, 'Look, you are a nice girl, but I don't think of you in that way. I mean … you are truly wonderful, but I really love Stuti. No matter how bad it is between us at this moment, I just cannot run away from that. I hope you understand. You are special and I know you'll find someone who'll love you more than I would have.'

Juhi's heart almost stopped beating before it began pounding. She was shattered and felt like her entire world had collapsed in a split second. They left soon after, and though she hated to cry, she bawled her eyes out after reaching home.

Abhay, if I could give you one thing in life, I would give you the ability to see yourself through my eyes. Only then will you realise how special you are to me. I feel dead inside. Have you no feelings for me? You mean you never loved me? Not even for a second? Then why did you give me hope by spending so much time with me? You wanted comfort after your break-up and you found that in me. Was that all there was between us? I really thought we had a connection. But now I feel I am a frequent wanderer in a land that exists only in my head. You broke my heart to such an extent that no one can heal it now. Now what? Is this the end? Abhay, I will lose a guy who never loved me. However, you will lose a girl who loved you with all her heart.

Six

The hardest thing to do is watch the one you love love someone else. It's said that you don't know what you have until it's gone. But what about Juhi, who already knew? She just had to sit there, watching Abhay helplessly as he walked away from her. Isn't that much worse? Being in the same space made things more difficult. Her confession of love hadn't affected him even a bit, and he behaved like he used to before with her and with everyone around. But what drove her insane was that Abhay and Stuti had patched up. What she didn't know was that not only had they patched up, they had decided to get married as well. Stuti's parents had come to Pune from Mumbai specially to meet Abhay and his family.

Abhay was getting ready for the occasion, wearing Stuti's favourite shirt. 'Mummy, they will be here in the next half an hour. Are we ready? Your snacks and welcome gifts?'

'Yes, Abhay, everything is ready. You just relax.'

'Abhay,' his dad called out, gesturing for him to sit beside him. 'I know you have told us already but I want to ask you again, you are sure about marrying Stuti, right?'

'Yes, Dad. I know what you are thinking and we have talked about it too. She earns more than me and is in a better position in a better organisation, but we are both fine with it. Our generation is much more rational than yours, Dad. Don't worry, please.'

Abhay made sure everything was in place before Stuti's family arrived. He then texted her, 'Listen, as I had told you, my parents are not flashy. They believe in simple living and have been like that their entire life. So, if they ask whether you would be comfortable staying with us after marriage, don't overreact at that time. Just say yes. Rest I will handle as we have decided.'

Stuti replied, 'But what if my parents say something? I am their only child and they would want to know how my life will be. Whether I will be staying with my in-laws or have a separate house. Also, you know it well, my dad is a reputed lawyer, so he has this habit of poking people and questioning them.' She sent a laughing emoji along with it.

'They'll come to know that their daughter is going to live the best life ahead,' Abhay replied with kisses.

When they arrived, Abhay treated them courteously. After the snacks were served, their parents settled down to chat. Abhay and Stuti were both a little nervous but it all went smoothly. 'Our kids have decided it already. We just have to take care of the formalities,' Stuti's dad said and sipped his tea.

'Yes, of course. That's the thing with this generation. But it's great as they are smart and independent and take their own decisions,' Abhay's dad said.

Stuti's mom joined in, 'You are right—we never had those choices.'

'Looks like she is regretting the decision to marry me.' Stuti's dad laughed aloud and the others joined in.

After some more discussion, Stuti's dad finally asked, 'Abhay, you tell me, do you have any expectations about the wedding ceremony?'

Abhay smiled. He looked towards Stuti for a brief moment and then said to her father, 'We just want our marriage day to be simple. I mean, by calling only a limited number of people, we can at least be attentive towards them. Anyway, most people are interested only in good food and sweets.'

'Ya, and we won't even know most of them. Instead, we can go for a tour of Europe, which would be awesome.'

Stuti's dad said, 'We don't want to wait too long. If you are fine with it, then we can arrange a date for next month itself.'

That came as a shocker for Abhay. His family seemed fine with it though, as anyway Abhay wanted to keep it simple.

Fuck, next month. That's too early. Let me stay a bachelor for at least half a year more. He looked at Stuti and realised from her expression that she knew what her father was going to suggest.

'I am sorry. I should have told you in the morning when I had a long debate with my family, but it would have panicked you,' Stuti texted Abhay.

He read it and sighed.

Their marriage was fixed for the twentieth of the next month! By the time they were done, it was lunchtime. Abhay insisted he would serve them and asked Stuti to join.

Abhay's mom stopped her, saying, 'No, you don't have to do that. Anyway, we women have to handle the kitchen after marriage.'

Stuti didn't react. Abhay had told her not to do so.

'It's okay, Aunty. You guys talk, and we will handle this.'

Abhay's mom smiled. She felt happy about Abhay's choice. They started laying the table and finding the opportunity in the kitchen, Abhay held Stuti by her waist from behind and said, 'So, Ms Stuti … you are soon going to be Mrs Stuti Abhay. How are you feeling?'

'I can't express it. It's exciting, but scary at the same time.' Stuti loosened his grip and turned.

'Ya, there are no break-ups after marriage. And your father is a lawyer anyway.' Abhay winked.

Stuti stood on her toes, took her face closer to his and whispered, 'Think again. Do you want to or do you still need time?'

'Hmmm …' Abhay gave a thoughtful look and said, 'Done, thought about it.'

'And what is it?'

'A yes,' he said, and leaned down to kiss her. He couldn't wait to spend the rest of his life with her.

• •

The most difficult thing in life is not to love or stay loyal, but to get over someone you love. Initially, Juhi pretended that she was fine though it was crushing her heart. She wanted desperately to regain her peace of mind but couldn't break out of her depression. She had always thought of herself as a strong person who was emotionally insulated. But now she frequently took days off from work, doing nothing but stay in her room. She would look at his pictures from the days they spent together, though that only made her feel more devastated.

You know what hurt me more, Abhay, more than your rejection? You didn't even bother to talk about it again. You pretended like it was just another casual evening for you. How easily you forgot that, when Stuti wasn't around, it was I who supported you and was with you. Now I know that those days meant nothing to you. A few words from your side would have made me feel better. But you never felt it necessary.

And then, as if reading her mind, Abhay came up to her one day. 'Are you all right? You seem lost since that day. I hope you didn't feel bad …'

'No, no, I am fine. I just had some health issues. That's it,' Juhi lied.

'Are you sure?'

'Absolutely.'

'Then how about a mastani today to make you feel better?' Abhay asked with a smile.

'I don't think it will work,' Juhi said instinctively, but immediately realised it was a clear giveaway of her feelings. 'I mean, I have stomach issues and it could get worse.'

'Oh, okay. Some other time then,' he said.

Juhi watched him leave. She wanted to go with him. But only if he had been hers. Only hers. She stared at her computer screen, controlling her tears. Karan called her to his desk after some time.

'How are you feeling now?' he asked.

'Better, thanks.'

Karan opened her performance report and showed it to her. 'Juhi, do you know that your last week's performance was impacted because of your days off? I know you will make up for it, but I hope you don't have to take more leave.'

'I seriously had health issues. And I was not able to login from home,' Juhi said.

Karan looked uncomfortable. He said, 'I just wanted to let you know that your performance ratings dropped, and I don't want you to lose track of things.'

'Karan, I will cover up. Don't worry. You can trust me,' she assured him, although she had no clue how she was going to do that when she knew she was not able to cope with her situation.

Nisha could not bear to see her in this condition and, in the evening, once they were home, she had a word with her.

'You have to stop being so helpless. This is taking you nowhere, and who are you doing it for? Abhay has blinded himself. You have to realise and accept that he loves someone else. And that's not in your control.' Nisha sat in front of her on her bed and gave her a cup of coffee.

Juhi took the cup from her and held it with both hands. She looked out of the window. 'Currently it seems like nothing is in my control. I know he loves someone but I also love him and I have never loved anyone this much.'

'But you are ruining your health,' Nisha said, and calmly pointed out the changes that she had seen in Juhi in the last few days. 'Look at your face. There are dark circles under your eyes and your face is so pale. You stay awake the whole night, you are hardly eating anything, and most of the time you are in your bedroom alone. You should come out with us instead, your friends. That will make you feel better when you look at yourself in the mirror.'

'And how should I make my soul look better? Do you have a solution for it?' Juhi looked back at her. But Nisha had an answer to it which was quite rational.

'Yes. Firstly, stop listening to those fucking sad break-up songs and delete that folder of his photos on your phone. You just cannot keep gazing at him. Neither is he a Marvel hero nor are you a psycho lover.'

Juhi looked at herself in the mirror on the wall. She contemplated the times she would listen to sad songs alone and said, 'You are right. Whenever I listen to those songs, it triggers all my emotions. You know, I want to meet the person who wrote *Ek tarfa pyaar ki takat kuch aur hoti hai, sirf mera haq hai ispe*. To fuck with the strength of one-side love, what the fuck should I do with it? Put it as toppings on pizza and eat it? The fact is, one-sided love hurts, and it hurts badly.'

'I think you need to chill. I have a plan and I'm not

asking you, I'm telling you—we're going clubbing. I'll call Gautam too,' Nisha said.

'Ya, you will take a free couple entry and I'll bloody pay for stag. Sometimes I feel I should have been like you. Carefree,' Juhi commented; even that made her sad.

'Now if you are done, get ready and we'll get going.'

No matter how much anyone consoles you, one-sided love makes you feel terrible. You may pretend to the world outside that it gives you strength, there are no commitments, no worries and you can just smile looking at your loved one. Accept it or not, when you know that they can never be yours, your heart aches.

• •

They reached the club an hour later and saw that Gautam was already there. He was with one of his friends, Rohit. He greeted Nisha with a hug and said, 'Sorry that I'm tagging along. When you made the plan all of a sudden, I was with Gautam and too bored to go back home. I hope you don't mind.'

'Of course not. Unless you plan to get dead drunk and we have to carry you back home!'

Rohit laughed and said, 'I am too hefty to be lifted.'

Gautam had reserved a table and once they all sat down, Nisha introduced Rohit and Juhi. Rohit saw Juhi wasn't in a great mood, and said, 'It's party time. Why are you looking so off—what happened?'

'Nothing,' Juhi said.

'Actually, she is going through a bad heartbreak,' Nisha said.

Annoyed, Juhi glared at Nisha, but before she could say anything, Rohit did.

'Oh, I see.' His expression had no sympathy in it. In a casual tone, he said, 'What's the big deal? I go through a heartbreak almost every month. It's tough when you finally recognise the true side of people.'

Nisha was amazed to hear that and asked, 'Then how do you cope with it?' She thought he could give some tips to Juhi.

'Good sex. That works.'

'Damn, you freak.' Nisha laughed.

The waiter interrupted their conversation. Nisha ordered drinks for everyone and some snacks and once they were on their own again, she continued the discussion.

'So, where were we. Oh ya ... sex—you were talking about sex,' Nisha said.

'Ya. It works great as closure; it helps you move on.'

He looked at Juhi, but she moved backwards, and said, 'That's great if it helps you. But don't try it on me. It's not going to work.'

'No, no, I am not trying anything on. I was just making a suggestion.'

Juhi faked a smile and turned towards Nisha. 'I want to have vodka.'

'Darling, are you sure you want to drink?' Nisha asked, surprised.

'Yes.' Juhi knew that wasn't the solution, but she wanted to run away from the demons inside her head.

Nisha didn't stop her. She wanted Juhi to find solace in something at least, and she thought maybe this would help.

But Nisha was wrong. It only made things worse. Juhi got drunk very quickly, and in that state called Abhay before Nisha could stop her. Juhi asked him to meet her right away. At first Abhay refused, saying he was already in bed, but Juhi insisted and Abhay eventually gave in. He sent her his live location and asked her to come in some time. She wanted to go alone, but Nisha wouldn't let her.

'Juhi, you are drunk. Please ride slowly,' Nisha screamed, sitting behind her on the Scooty. 'You shouldn't even be riding!'

'I have to talk to him. I know I can convince him to be with me. I am a better choice for him.' Juhi's voice made it evident that she was drunk, and Nisha feared that even Abhay would notice it. She was nervous about what was going to happen.

After a few minutes, they were at his building. Abhay came down and walked across the street to the other side where they were standing.

'What's the matter?' he asked in a groggy voice. It was already midnight.

Tears rolled down Juhi's face as she said, 'You really have no feelings for me? We had such a good time together when Stuti wasn't around. Those six weeks were the best days of my life and I thought that we had something special. I thought we were more than just good friends. We shared such a lovely bond, supported each other and understood each other. You too loved my company. Didn't you?'

Abhay saw that she wasn't able to stand straight and even her tone wasn't normal. 'Are you drunk?' he asked. He looked at Nisha, who was standing next to Juhi. 'Nisha what is happening?'

'I really love you, Abhay. No one can love you like I do. Believe me. You told me to get over it and I tried, but it's not happening. I need you. I can't live without you. I don't know how I should prove my love; only I know what you mean to me.'

Juhi wanted to hug Abhay right there and even stepped forward, but Abhay held her and said, 'Juhi, you are a nice girl, really. Like I said, I am sure you will find someone good. And he will be really lucky to be with you. But that man isn't me.'

'Why?' she cried. 'Take your time, but don't just reject me without even giving it a try.'

'Juhi, why don't you understand that I can't be with you.' Abhay took a deep breath and said, 'I love Stuti.'

'Yes. He loves me and we are getting married,' Stuti said, coming up to them. She had overheard Abhay's last words. She folded her arms, clearly furious to see Juhi there. 'Our marriage is fixed. So, will you stop all this nonsense and buzz off from our lives? You're insane.'

Juhi was taken aback for a second to see Stuti. Being sober had stopped her from saying what she wanted to Stuti, and now she blurted it out.

'Abhay is mine. Not yours. What are you doing here?'

'Excuse me. I should be the one asking you that. You are standing near *my* house. And Abhay and I are *engaged*.'

Juhi ignored her. She turned to Abhay and said, almost pleadingly, 'Abhay ... I love you.'

'Bitch, can you just go away?' Stuti screamed and stepped closer. The rage was visible in her eyes.

Nisha asked her to calm down. Abhay too pulled her back and said, 'Stuti, let me handle it.' He requested Nisha, 'Please take her away right now. We will talk later.'

But Juhi was not in her senses and continued to talk. 'It's me who understands him, not you. Do you even care for his dreams? I know you have a superiority complex. I'm the one who will keep him happy, not you.'

Stuti raised her arm to slap Juhi, but Abhay held her back, gripping her wrist tight.

Juhi didn't stop there, though, despite Nisha telling her to. Under the effect of alcohol, she expressed all that she had suppressed in her heart for so long. 'I am not a bitch ... you are a bitch who doesn't value his love.'

Abhay couldn't take her words anymore; the threshold of his patience had been reached. 'Stop it now. Enough. Just go away. You'll never get what you want. Mind my words, you will never get what you want. You have lost the plot. Leave, right now.'

Nisha apologised to Abhay on Juhi's behalf and took her away, riding the Scooty herself. They didn't speak with each other till they reached their apartment. Nisha cursed herself for not stopping Juhi, but she'd had no idea things would get so out of hand.

'I will not let Abhay live with her; I'll make sure that it won't happen.' Those were the last words from Juhi before she crashed out.

Sometimes, all the love in the world is not enough to save something. Had Juhi hit rock bottom after what had just happened? Or did she really mean what she had just said? If so, then it could knock her down even further till the sky became a mere speck.

Seven

Juhi wasn't herself when she let her emotions out, but if she had not been drunk, she would have never conveyed them at all. With alcohol, her inhibitions melted away. The only problem was, the following day, when she was sober, she stood by her decision to not let Abhay live with Stuti. She was hesitant to face Abhay after what she had done, but she wanted to break their relationship, by hook or by crook.

When she told Nisha about it, her friend immediately said she wasn't in favour of it. Nisha gave her lemon juice and said, 'You are still having a terrible hangover. You haven't had alcohol before and it happens. It makes us illogical and we lose the ability to judge what's right and wrong. But now at least you should be thinking rationally.'

'Look, I know I crossed a line yesterday. I just wanted to tell him that I am better for him. But Abhay didn't care at all. He even said that I will never get what I want in life. It made me feel like a loser.'

Juhi hadn't registered the words when Stuti revealed they were getting married, but in the morning, she could clearly hear Stuti announcing they were engaged. That broke her heart all over again.

'I was there, you don't need to repeat what happened. You have told me this a hundred times already. But let bygones be bygones. That cannot justify what you are up to. That's not who you are.' Nisha didn't want any further complications. She cared for Juhi and didn't want her to hurt herself any more.

'I just want him to realise my true love for him.'

'Whatever it is, you are not a troublemaker and you shouldn't behave like one. I am not with you in this. I strongly feel you should let things go. You think that you will win over his love by forcing it? Why don't you get it—it's not you,' Nisha yelled at her.

I know that's not me. I know I am not the kind of person who can hurt anyone. But Abhay, you are forcing me to take on a personality. I am not a loser and I want you to know that. You hurt me and, sadly, breaking someone's heart isn't a crime.

Juhi was not convinced a bit by Nisha. You can stop someone when they aren't aware of right and wrong. But how can you stop someone who knows it already and still wants to take that dark path?

Juhi consistently came home late for the next two days after office and didn't tell Nisha where she had gone. For the third day in a row, she asked Nisha to go home alone as she had some work. Nisha knew she was up to something, but it was out of her control. She just asked her to take care and left. Juhi rode to the same location Abhay had sent her and parked the Scooty in a by-lane.

She had been doing the same thing for the last couple of days so she could keep an eye on Stuti's movements. She had found out what time she reached home and, more importantly, her flat number. She was going to put a letter in Stuti's letterbox. Today was the day that she was going to do that. She stood outside the gate and kept a watch on the security guard. After an hour or so, she saw him going to a paan shop and she quickly went inside and walked towards the letterboxes. She put a letter in Stuti's letterbox and walked away without anyone noticing her.

When Stuti returned from work, she checked the letterbox as she did every evening and saw the letter inside. On the envelope was written, *'From Your Well-Wisher'*.

She was perplexed but was so tired that she didn't read it immediately. It was only when she was about to sleep that her eyes fell on the letter, which she had kept on the bedside table. She opened the envelope, lay on the bed, and started reading.

Stuti, this is important. Please read carefully and decide for yourself.

Your to-be husband, Abhay, is faking his love for you. He is a cheat. You are not the first to fall for his act. He has done it with a few girls before and even now he is setting a trap for you. He will promise you that he will marry you, but won't by giving some reason or the other. I am sure he made you meet his family too; that's how he tricks girls. And once he is tired of you, he will switch to some other girl. How do I know all this? Because I was also one of his victims. Now, you will get an urge to call him and talk about this letter, but that would be your biggest mistake. He'll figure out a good lie to tell you and it's only you who is going to suffer. You have been with him for just over a year. He played with my feelings for a couple of years and had promised me the same things he's promised you. If you think I am playing a prank and none of it is true, then that is your decision. But if you believe me, then meet me tomorrow evening near the building that is under construction in the lane next to yours.

Stuti was shocked. She could not figure out who could have written this letter. She trusted Abhay, but for some reason, she didn't want to tell him about this. She stopped herself from doing it and the next day, when she met him, she said, 'Can I ask you something?' The letter was on her mind constantly.

'Sure,' Abhay said, leaning forward to kiss her.

She pushed him back and said, 'I know this is out of the blue, but I want to know what went wrong with your ex-girlfriend.'

'What?' Abhay raised his eyebrows in surprise. He hadn't expected that.

Stuti continued. 'You told me you both loved each other and wanted to get married, then what happened?'

'Why do you want to dig into my past all of a sudden?' Abhay's expression didn't change.

'I don't know, the question is haunting me from yesterday. Please, I want to know.'

Abhay picked up the water bottle in front of him and took a sip. Stuti waited for him to speak. He took a deep breath and said, 'I found out she was cheating on me. I got to know through our common friend. Initially, I didn't believe him. I thought she was honest in our relationship. I thought she loved me wholeheartedly. But when I saw it myself, I didn't think twice before breaking up with her. I read some texts she'd sent the other guy, and that made it clear. That was it,' Abhay said. 'Now, may I ask, what made you bring this up?'

'Nothing. I was just remembering the moments we have spent together, our talks, and I recalled you mentioning your ex.' Stuti smiled, but her thoughts were still on the letter. She probed further to find out more details.

'So, had she met your family?'

Abhay wasn't comfortable talking about it, but to clear her mind, he answered. 'Not officially, but yes, they knew that we were dating, that I loved her, and wanted to settle down soon. But it didn't happen. And then you came into my life and I felt I would have made a mistake if I had married her. Whatever happens happens for the best.'

Stuti remained silent. Even she didn't know what was stopping her from telling him the truth. Somewhere in her mind, she thought that if it were related to Juhi, Abhay would never confront Juhi about it. She knew that wasn't his nature; he had always been passive. Thus, she felt she should sort it out on her own to clear any doubts.

The next day, Stuti reached the location mentioned in the letter and waited for some time. There weren't many people around, but she looked at every other person passing by, wondering if this was the one who was behind it. After waiting for more than an hour, Stuti decided to dismiss the incident as a prank and left.

Juhi had decided not to go. She had planned to reach there after office, but went home instead. Sitting in her bedroom alone, she looked at the wedding invitation card Abhay had posted on Instagram.

Abhay weds Stuti.

It brought tears to her eyes.

What am I doing? Why I am doing this? I wasn't ready to let you go. I wanted to tell Stuti to stay away from you. I know it wouldn't have been easy, but I thought what I'd written in the letter might convince her. But today, when I was about to do what I intended, I realised that's not how I want to have you in my life. Nisha was right. I can't let obsession win over my love. It's not a game where I will do anything to win. I will never understand why the things we want the most aren't always meant to be. As I sit here, wiping tears from my red, swollen eyes, I finally understand that you will never be mine. Time after time, I tried to convince myself to hold on to fragments of hope that you would choose me. Because facing the truth is not a truth I wish to know. I have fought with myself to express my love and now I am fighting to let you go. I am worn out. I am exhausted from all that fighting and I won't do it anymore. I just can't. Because nothing will ever change. I am just feeding my heart with fantasies. And that's exactly what one-sided love feels like. It's like paying a penance for something I haven't done. You were on my mind 24/7, but I know that you don't think about me. I would check my phone repeatedly, waiting for your call that rarely came. I sent you messages with so much excitement, just to receive a short reply from you. I was unable to take my eyes off you, but you hardly noticed my soul. I silenced my intuition when I knew I should listen to it the most. There was nothing I wanted more than to keep it, keep us, together, but I have finally realised that I am alone in all of this and there's nothing I can do about it.

That was it. Rock bottom. She could sense it, not knowing what it would take to not stay there. She had to come to terms with reality. And the reality was that Abhay would be getting married to Stuti, and Juhi was left helpless and hopeless.

Eight

'In the entire population of India, I loved just one guy, and even he didn't love me back. Isn't it scary?' Juhi had got a bottle of vodka home and was drinking along with Nisha and Gautam. She was trying to restore peace in her life. It was around eleven o'clock at night and she was playing music loudly to shut out the thoughts of him that haunted her.

'I have an idea. Let's date each other, even I am bored of my boyfriend,' Nisha said. She looked at Gautam and made a teasing face. 'He irritates me a lot these days. What say, Juhi? Isn't that cool? No fucking boys in our lives. And anyway we are already living together.'

Juhi screamed, 'No … Gautam is too cute for you …' Juhi got up from her place and hugged him. 'Gautam, you are the best boyfriend.'

Gautam turned to Nisha and said, 'See, everyone accepts it but you don't. So ungrateful!'

'Aww … don't be sad, baby,' Nisha said and laughed. 'Come, give me a hug. I know you are the best.'

Nisha embraced him. Gautam brought his lips closer

to hers and planted a kiss. They became so engrossed that they forgot that Juhi was around.

After a moment, she said, 'Guys, can you stop your PDA please? It makes me feel even more lonely. No love, no sex, no romance, no pampering. Sometimes I feel Abhay was right. I'll never get what I want.'

'He was just full of nonsense. You should listen to me. Start dating someone and you will feel better. It's the best thing to help you move on.'

'Now which doctor suggested that to you?'

'That's Dr Nisha's therapy. And it works.' Nisha bowed, as if she had given her a break-up mantra.

Juhi rolled her eyes and picked up her phone to check her notifications. There was one Instagram pop up about Abhay saying he had uploaded a photo. She clicked on it and was redirected to his Instagram profile. She saw his honeymoon picture and all the stories that he had uploaded.

'Abhay has gone to the Maldives for his honeymoon,' Juhi said. 'He has uploaded a photo from the resort. All his stories are full of their pictures. Selfie in bathrobes, selfie in the pool, selfie in swimsuits, selfie cuddling on the bed. Bloody shameless creatures.'

Nisha tried to snatch her phone, but Juhi pulled it away. 'Why don't you just block him instead of stalking his profile?' Nisha said.

'I did. But within ten minutes I unblocked him as I wanted to see his updates.' More than anyone else, Juhi was upset with herself for not able to remove him from her life.

'And what do you get from that?' Nisha asked, wanting to make her realise that it was pointless, but Juhi had an answer.

'When I abuse that bitch, I feel relaxed. The same feeling that you get after one hell of an aromatherapy spa. My mind is mollified,' Juhi said and began looking at their photos again. 'Let me leave a comment that they can qualify for Bhojpuri porn and should go for auditions.'

Nisha managed to snatch her phone this time. 'No, stop it. Don't do all that. It won't look good. And I don't want you to repeat what you did the last time you got drunk.'

Juhi jumped up and tried to grab Nisha's phone. 'Then if *you* comment it will look good. Give me your phone. Anyway, how will it matter to you.' She tried to snatch it but Nisha was too quick for her.

Gautam, watching all the drama, instantly hid his phone before she could try and take his. The doorbell came to the rescue. Nisha opened the door and saw the security guard outside. He tried to peep in to see what was happening inside. Nisha glared at him and, seeing this, the security guard said, 'Sorry, madam. Actually, I got a few complaints from the neighbours that the music is too loud. Please if you can lower the volume ...'

Juhi heard this and walked to the door. 'Who the fuck is complaining? Tell them to get lost,' she said, and then added, 'Do you want to come and drink with us? Anyway you always check me out.'

'No ... no.'

'Bhaiya, please leave,' Nisha said.

But Juhi continued, 'Don't get scared. Tell me the truth. Do you want to go out with me? My friend said that's the best therapy.'

The guard gave a smile and Nisha snapped her fingers in front of his face and shouted, 'Oh hello, control your thoughts. And please leave. I will lower the volume. Just don't tell anyone what you just saw. Else you know me well.'

'Don't worry, madam. Just that …' Nisha understood what he wanted and handed a hundred rupee note to him. She had always done that so he wouldn't tell the owner or society members what they did or who visited. Nisha closed the door and led Juhi to her bedroom to make her sleep.

'Abhay, you are driving me crazy. And the sound of the waves is making me feel more erotic. Please don't make me wait anymore,' Stuti moaned.

'Whenever I see you in such a mood, your expressions arouse me and bring out my wild side.'

'Oh Abhay … stop talking and just come here. I need you right now,' Stuti pulled him over and removed his bathrobe.

Abhay pressed his lips softly against hers. She surrendered herself to him. Gazing at her for a while after breaking the kiss, he pressed his forehead against hers, feeling her hot breath against his skin. It felt perfect. He threw her bathrobe on the sofa nearby and whispered to her softly, 'You are too hot to handle.'

'And you are my hunk. Now get going.' Stuti scratched his back in ecstasy.

She dug her nails into his back every time he sped up. She felt surreal, magical and Abhay took her to the highest peak of ecstasy.

'How was it; the first time after marriage?' Abhay asked as he collapsed beside her on the bed.

'You were never this passionate before. I love how you handle me in bed.' Stuti ran her fingers though his hair.

'And you never moaned so loudly before this. If we were back home, I'm sure our neighbours would have had a bad night listening to your melodies.'

'I love you so much, Abhay.'

'I love you too, Juhi. I really love you a lot. I am sorry I couldn't confess it in front of Stuti that day, but you make me feel so good, and today, you pleasured me like never before. I love you, Juhi.'

Juhi woke up in a terrible state. She was sweating and her body trembled. She had fantasised that Abhay was making love to her. For a moment, she couldn't differentiate between her dream and reality and felt it was actually happening when Abhay said her name. She felt dehydrated and, after having a couple of glasses of water, tried to get back to sleep.

I can't let him dominate my feelings. I just can't. He is still controlling me and I am letting him do that. I have to release myself from his memories and move on. He is happy in his life; why shouldn't I be? I have made up my mind—Abhay, your chapter is over.

• •

Juhi got up at noon with the vibration of her phone. It was a text message from Arpit.

'Free for brunch today?'

Juhi didn't reply. She got up and opened the door of her bedroom. Nisha and Gautam had ordered pizza to make her feel better.

'Here's your favourite pizza, Juhi. We were just waiting for you. Wash up and we will pounce on it,' Nisha said, sprinkling oregano on the pizza and pouring out water in glasses.

Juhi yawned and sat on the chair. She felt lighter in her head after so many days. She asked Nisha, 'Did you tell Arpit about Abhay?'

Nisha kept the bottle aside and said, 'Why would I? Now what mess have you got into?'

'Nothing! He messaged asking if I am free for brunch today.'

'That's superb. I think you should go. You'll feel better,' Nisha suggested.

'I know why you're saying that.'

'Ya? Why?' Nisha asked.

'Because you want to have my portion of pizza too.' Juhi took a bite of the pizza. 'Hmm ... it's delicious.'

'Aah ... that's a different story. But wasn't that the second tip in the article you read about getting over heartbreak? Go on a date and make new memories?'

Juhi laughed. 'No, that was the third.'

Nisha kept the pizza aside and told her seriously, 'I think you should go. Get over Abhay now. Take it as a learning experience and I am sure that after the storm passes, you will be so much wiser, strong and confident about yourself and life.'

'Nisha is right,' Gautam agreed. 'Take this time to find out who you are. Don't let this experience take away your shine. She isn't telling you to fall in love again. A date won't do any harm.'

'I know. Even I am fed up of crying again and again. In fact, last night, I decided that I won't think of Abhay again. Ever.' Juhi picked up her phone and texted Arpit, saying she would meet him.

'Great! See you at Marriot in an hour?' Arpit replied.

'There could be nothing better than this. I'm so glad,' Nisha said, hugging Juhi. 'Now go and get ready. Leave this pizza for us. Your pizza is waiting at Marriot hotel.'

'Fuck off. I am not giving up any of my pizza. Anyway, why should I be weight conscious now. I'll eat whatever I want, whenever I feel. I'll finish this and then leave.'

While Juhi had agreed to go on a date with Arpit, she was clear that it was casual. She wore her favourite pink top and dark jeans and applied light make-up. After a long time, she felt good looking at herself in the mirror. She realised now, how much she had stopped loving and caring for herself.

When she reached Marriot, Arpit was outside waiting for her. They walked into the hotel and settled down in the restaurant. Juhi felt like her mind was clouded with nothing in particular and yet, at the same time, with everything at once.

They had their lunch and Arpit didn't realise how time flew. 'Are you also going to say something, or is it just me who is going to speak?' he said with a wide smile.

She shook her head slightly; his words had taken her back in time. Even Abhay had said the same thing to her.

I had decided that I will move on, I will not think of Abhay. But, in every moment, I am searching for Abhay's traits in Arpit. What is wrong with me? But she couldn't stop herself from thinking, *Arpit is a nice guy ... but he is not Abhay.*

She met his eyes across the table and said with a smile, 'The food here is amazing.'

Arpit nodded and looked away, gazing casually at the other people around. Juhi watched how he sucked in his right cheek slightly, as if restricting himself from saying whatever was occupying his mind.

'What?' Juhi asked, curious.

'Can we go for a drive later, if you don't mind?' He looked nervous.

'Sure.' Juhi smiled, but deep inside, her thoughts made her unstable. She wasn't able to stop comparing him with Abhay.

The restaurant was thinning out, and it was only then that she noticed the silence in the place. They decided to leave. When the valet brought the car, Arpit opened the door for her. He went to the driving seat and, after tipping the valet, drove away swiftly.

His eyes glistened in the light that entered through the windows; it made the intensity of his glances at her so much more intimate. She blinked twice and looked down.

The feelings that had been stirred up in the pit of her stomach were unbearable.

'Juhi, you look beautiful. I didn't expect that you would come out with me, but let me tell you, you made my day.' He smiled.

'Thanks, I needed this badly. My life has been hellish recently.' Juhi smiled back.

'I know how you must be feeling. Don't worry, I'll be with you.' He reached over and took her hand.

Juhi knew how much it hurt when hopes were shattered—it wasn't too long back when she had been in Arpit's position. She didn't want to send a wrong message and thus clarified before he could think otherwise.

'Arpit ... I know where this is heading. But I don't want any more complications in my life. I hope you understand.' She gently extracted her hand from his and continued, 'I am already going through a lot and all I want right now is peace. I want to get back to my own self.'

Arpit laughed and said, 'Chill. It's not what you are thinking. Trust me.'

'Okay, great,' Juhi said, determined to enjoy the drive with Arpit. She didn't want to ruin the day with negative emotions.

• •

'Drinks are on me today, so have one more round,' Nisha said to Juhi. They were at their regular club.

Juhi ordered her fourth peg of vodka and asked Nisha, 'Why? Did you fight with Gautam?'

Nisha laughed. 'No. He's not here because I told him no boys today.'

Nisha had been drinking cautiously and was sober. She didn't want any ruckus that night knowing Juhi was going to get drunk. Nisha munched on a French fry and said, 'I thought Arpit was going to try his luck with you knowing there's no Abhay in your life now. Strange, he didn't.'

Juhi replied, 'I must say that I had a good time with him. But he's not my type.'

'And what is your type?' Nisha asked and then immediately realised she shouldn't have asked that question. She quickly continued, 'What about that guy? He's hot. Don't you think so?'

Juhi looked to where Nisha was indicating. 'Ya, he's kinda cute.'

'Oops, he saw you looking at him,' Nisha said.

'Oh no!' Juhi said.

'I'm sure he will be at our table in the next few minutes.'

Juhi didn't ask her how she knew this. Instead, she said, 'And I know what will be your next statement. Flirt with him, it's good for your health, right?'

'And I know what you will say,' Nisha mimicked her. 'I am not into all this. Don't try it on me.'

Juhi laughed and kept her glass aside. She leaned closer to her and whispered, 'For a change, I am going to try it this time.'

Nisha's eyes almost popped out. 'No … you are not serious, right?'

Juhi gave her a naughty smile, and that look only scared Nisha. 'Please don't create any trouble tonight. I beg you. If you do it, I am not going to let you drink from now on.'

Just then, the guy they had looked at came over to them and said, 'Hi, I'm Sumit. And you are ...'

'I am Juhi, and she is Nisha.'

'You girls are alone?' he asked.

'How can two people be alone? Are you so drunk that you see us as one?' Nisha said.

He laughed and shook his head. He turned to Juhi and said, 'Would you like to dance?'

Juhi readily got up and headed with him to the dance floor. They began to dance, their feet like the waters of a waterfall: swift and vibrant and full of energy. With every step, she felt she was pushing Abhay away from her and finding her true self. Her hair fell over her eyes, like a curtain blocking out sunlight. She lifted her hand to brush away her hair, and he reached out and held on to it. She carefully lay her hand on Sumit's shoulder and her eyes twinkled back at him in invitation. She took her face close to his and she whispered, 'You know how to be romantic.'

He blushed and asked, 'Are you single?'

'Absolutely. What about you?'

'Was in a relationship. But now there's no one. At least till this moment.'

Juhi smiled and said, 'Even I just moved on. But I wasn't in a relationship. It was a one-sided affair.'

'Let's celebrate our singlehood tonight. What say?' he whispered in her hair as they danced.

'Why not?'

'Not here. Let's go on a drive.'

The next moment, Juhi was in front of Nisha, convincing her that she was sober enough to make this decision.

'How can I believe you?' Nisha said. She was uncomfortable about leaving her alone with a random guy.

'Am I stalking Abhay or even talking about him? No, right? Then tell me, why do you think that I am not sober.'

'I am afraid it isn't safe, Juhi. Just finish it off here and let's leave in some time,' Nisha suggested.

'On other days you want me to try all the thrilling things in life and now when I am doing it, you are scared. I can also figure out people; I agree, I'm not as great as you, but I'm not that naïve either. He is a sweet guy. I will be back home in some time.'

Juhi eventually managed to convince Nisha and left with Sumit. But though she had told Nisha she wasn't drunk, she actually was.

She sat in Sumit's car and they drove along the lanes of Pune. After chatting for some time, he asked, 'Do you want to drink some more?' He stopped the car on the side of a quiet road.

'I don't mind, but where would we get anything now?' Juhi asked.

'I am always stocked up.' Sumit leaned over and pulled out a bag from the backseat.

'What are we waiting for then?' Juhi said.

Sumit took out a bottle of vodka from the bag and poured some into a Bisleri bottle, along with Sprite.

They drank in the car, and after some time, Juhi could feel her vision blurring. The next thing she knew, she was waking up in a hotel room, alone. She got up from the bed with a jerk and saw on the side table clock that it was eight o'clock. Juhi was shocked; she looked around, wondering how she had got to this room. Sumit was nowhere to be seen. She looked around for her phone and finally found it lying by the bed. She saw multiple missed calls and messages from Nisha and Gautam.

Oh my God, Nisha must have been so worried the whole night! She held her pounding head.

Juhi then saw that there was a notification from Google Pay too, that gave her goose bumps. She saw she had accepted a request for a money transfer and her saving account balance was nil. When she called that number, she found that it was switched off.

Fuck, fuck. This can't be real. When did I accept this? I don't remember anything. Her brain froze. Her hands and feet went cold.

She looked for her handbag everywhere but couldn't find it. Her life had turned upside down in one night. She could not believe she'd made the decision to go alone with that guy. She ran down to the reception, hoping to find out something about him. She was told by the person there that the room was booked in her name, and the room charges had been paid with her card when they checked in. It was a shady hotel, she could see, and when she enquired about CCTV, they informed her that their CCTV wasn't working. She had no way of getting information about the guy. She felt so broken, she just wanted to scream out loud. Her head spun like her world was going to end; her heart was beating so loud, it felt like it would burst soon. Juhi called Nisha, who told her to come home immediately and booked a cab for her. On her way home, she tried to remember what had happened.

Her clouded memory got a bit clear. She remembered they were drinking in the car and he leaned forward to kiss her. Then she had agreed to his suggestion that they go a hotel room instead of making out in the car. She also remembered that they drank a lot in the room too; at least, she did.

'You are so gorgeous, Juhi, you are driving me crazy. Your lips are so tender soft.'

'Oh, Abhay, I so want you right now. You are the best thing that happened to me.' Had she really called him Abhay? She couldn't believe she'd done that.

A brief memory of last night flashed in front of her eyes.

'Hey, Juhi. I need to make a payment of a thousand rupees urgently. Can you do it for me? My phone battery is dead.'

She tried hard, but couldn't recollect anything more than that. She felt completely desolate. She hadn't just lost Abhay, she had lost everything—her hope, and her entire self!

Nine

It's said that you are just one decision away from a totally different life. And Juhi's decision to go alone with Sumit was that one decision for her. Now, she had taken another—she had decided to leave Pune forever. Apart from her experience with Sumit, she had heard that Abhay was about to re-join office in a couple of days, and she felt she couldn't cope with being in the same space as him. This city, which had once given her peace of mind and a sense of power to achieve her goals now made her feel depressed and alone.

I wanted to grow big in the city, I had plans and was sure that I would achieve it. I had promised Dad that I would never let him down. But I have. I hope he will understand. After all, I am his daughter. And even if he doesn't, I'll make him understand. But this city is no more mine. I don't belong here anymore. Abhay, it's time to move entirely away from your life. It's enough now.

Juhi sent in her resignation. Since she had leave saved, she had decided to use that for her notice period and head home immediately. Nisha and Gautam were upset about her decision and had tried to convince her to stay back. But Juhi had made up her mind.

'Will you not reconsider this?' Nisha said, trying for the last time even though Juhi's flight would take off in a few hours.

Juhi shook her head. She zipped up the bag she was packing and weighed it to make sure it wasn't overweight.

'I shouldn't have let you go with that guy. Don't blame yourself and make this drastic decision.'

'It's not just about that night.' Juhi made her sit on the bed and, holding her by her shoulders said, 'I just need some time for myself. I have to move on.'

'But why are you going back? Moving on doesn't mean you should just leave everything. You can look for another job. I don't think this is the right decision,' Nisha said.

'Things are not that simple anymore, where one can decide what's right and what's wrong. I know that even switching jobs won't make me feel better if I am in the same city.'

Gautam saw Nisha looking at him with hope, so he said, 'I am there with you, Nisha is with you, then what do you fear? Just forget what has happened in the past.'

But nothing could change Juhi's mind. 'If it was so easy to forget, I would have done that long back. And you guys will be with me for my entire life, I know that.' Juhi stood up and hugged both of them. 'I am going to miss you. You guys stay happy and come to my village someday. I will show you the real India. And you can romance in my fields against a background of cows and buffalos.'

Nisha laughed, but there were tears in her eyes.

Juhi was equally emotional. Nisha was her everything from the time they had started living together. But she had left herself with no choice.

As the cab took her to the airport, she bid a final goodbye to Pune, wondering what awaited her as she unfolded a new page of her life.

• •

Juhi's parents were happy to have her back, but her father sensed that she was keeping something to herself. She had told them she had quit her job, but he found it odd that she had left work so abruptly. He could also see that she wasn't the same Juhi who used to be high spirited. She had lost a part of herself. For a couple of days, he waited to see if she would share what had happened, but she didn't. He didn't question her though. He wanted to give her space and time for herself until she felt comfortable about revealing the truth.

One evening, at dinner, her mother said, 'Now that you have no plans of going back, I will find a good boy for you and get you married. Then you can go to whichever city you want with him. I have no objections.'

Annoyed, Juhi kept her plate aside and said, 'Maa, please. I am not in a state to argue and discuss marriage here. I need my space. Can I get that in my home at least?'

Her mother had always been stubborn in her beliefs though, and now she refused to budge. 'Listen, if you have to stay here in this town, you can't just stay like this. You are crossing the right age to get married. People will start talking. They'll start making up stories about why you are back home all of a sudden. And I don't want people to point fingers at us and say we didn't give you the right upbringing.'

'Why does everything come down to only one thing—marriage,' Juhi raised her voice. 'I am not ready for it.'

But the discussion didn't end there. Her mother stuck to her point, and Juhi stopped arguing. The next evening, when her father was alone on the terrace, she walked up to him. She didn't mention the incident with Sumit, but told him what had happened with Abhay and that it was the reason she had quit her job and returned.

Her dad took her in his arms and consoled her. 'When you were a kid and used to fall off the cycle and get hurt, or whenever you didn't score good marks, you used to come to me and cry. And I would tell you that you will face many such disappointments in life, but you can't give up. I am just glad that nothing has changed in all these years—that you still feel like you can come to me and cry.'

Juhi had a special place in her heart for her dad that no one else could ever have. She hugged him with moist eyes. She knew her dad would hear her pain and wouldn't judge her. He would realise what his daughter was going through.

Her father continued. 'I could have held your hand each and every time but I didn't as I wanted you to find your own way. You used to tell me that whatever happens, I will never let you down. Your Maa thinks that you are a rebel who doesn't live a life like other girls in our town. But I know that you are ambitious and living that other life would go against your heart. She doesn't know that it's me who has always wanted you to be ambitious and instilled those qualities in you. I know that you will overcome this phase too.'

Juhi wiped her tears and sat with him, looking at the stars above. She could see herself in one of them. The one that didn't shine brightly but had that ability to do so. 'Dad, I need some time alone. I want to let go of my past. Totally. Please, I hope at least you understand.'

Juhi's father looked at her. He could see there was a little life back in her eyes after his words. 'What do you want me to do? Tell me what's going on in your mind.'

She said, 'I am looking for another job, but you know how bad things are in the economy. There are no openings right now. Once I get a good job, I want to continue working. But till then, let me stay here and help you and Suyash in your work. Please.'

'You know that girls don't work in the fields here. It's considered a man's job,' he said.

'I know, but you aren't like other parents who stop their daughters from doing what they want.'

Juhi's dad smiled and agreed to her request and that made her spirits lift. She felt hopeful again—to live and to survive! To be happy and to be what she wanted!

• •

Months passed, and Juhi began to feel herself recovering slowly. She hadn't been able to get a good job but kept trying. She worked hard with Suyash and her dad, putting her MBA brain to work. Her mother too was pacified with thoughts of getting her married soon.

In the other world, Abhay and Stuti continued to live in Stuti's apartment. Stuti had been promoted to general manager and Abhay worked in the same company. He was now on the same project as Nisha.

It was Stuti's birthday, and Abhay had got up early to receive the flowers that he had ordered online. When Stuti got up, he stood in front of her with the bouquet of flowers.

'Happy birthday, my love. I will do all that is in my power to put a smile on your face.'

Stuti was overwhelmed to see the decorations in the room and the flowers in his hand.

'Thank you, baby. When did you do all this? I can't believe I was so deeply asleep.'

Abhay kissed her, cuddled up to her on the bed and gazed into her eyes. He said without breaking eye contact, 'But this is not all I have in store for you. This year, I wanted to go bigger than a little note with roses and bigger even than lunch somewhere. I felt like planning a surprise for you, and that's when I thought I would take you on a drive. But I am not going to tell you the destination now. We will leave in the evening, so come back early from office. I have to plan a few things, and I have already applied for leave today.'

'You are too sweet. I love the way you pamper me. I'll come early.' She ruffled his hair and got up to get ready.

Abhay had booked a table at an exclusive and romantic rooftop restaurant, and asked for the background to be decorated especially for the occasion. After Stuti left, he made a call to confirm the arrangements. He was excited for the evening, especially because, in the past few weeks, since Stuti had become general manager, she hadn't been able to spend much time with Abhay. He was eager to relive the time that they used to spend together before marriage—carefree and without worrying about the tensions of life. Around six o'clock, he called Stuti, but she didn't answer it. A minute later she messaged that she was in a meeting and would be leaving soon. Abhay waited, but his wait didn't end. Stuti hadn't returned even by nine o'clock, and her phone was switched off. He tried calling at her office desk, but she didn't answer that either. It wasn't the first time this was happening. Repeatedly, she had started ignoring her personal life, giving priority to her work.

Abhay cancelled the dinner eventually, thoroughly disheartened. He opened a bottle of Scotch and poured himself a drink. As he sipped on it, he thought, *Sometimes I feel like I am the only one in this relationship. And I know that if I told her how I feel, she would yell at me saying I am not as ambitious as her. Are ambition and career more important than a relationship? Not to me, at least. I understand that it is important to her, but what about us? I put so much thought into this plan, just for her, and she didn't turn up. The day is special for me. I love her. And I know even she loves me, a lot, but I fear her ambition will come between us.*

His mind was so occupied he didn't realise that Stuti had come home. He immediately got up to speak to her, but when he saw her face, he felt concerned. She wasn't looking good, and seeing that, he made her sit on the bed in their room.

'Are you okay, what happened?' All his anger vanished within seconds.

Stuti didn't react but just looked at him.

'Tell me,' he said again.

Stuti got up from the bed and walked a few steps away from him. 'I'm pregnant.'

'Oh my God. Are you sure?' Abhay said.

'Yes. I've been feeling nauseous for a few days, and even vomited a couple of times. So, today I got a test and checked in the office after my meeting.'

Abhay's happiness knew no bounds and his heart pumped faster in joy. 'It was me who had planned surprises for you and you gave me the best surprise I could ever have. I love you so much, Stuti,' he said, letting the feeling sink in. 'I can't believe I'm going to be a father!'

Stuti moaned into her hands as she slumped down onto the bed. 'This changes everything. Things will never go back to how they are. How will I concentrate on my career? I just got promoted—how will I do my job properly now?'

Abhay squeezed her shoulder gently. 'I know things won't be same but try and think of the positives. You will soon be a mother. I am so happy right now.' Abhay was so excited, he didn't notice the look on Stuti's face.

'What positive? I am not ready for this now,' Stuti spat out.

'Calm down, Stuti. You know there's always good in every situation. And once you get used to the idea, you'll realise that soon we'll have a little one of our own that we have to take care of. It's a new beginning in our married life.'

'But I don't want a kid right now!' Stuti howled.

'Breathe, just think of the little darling growing inside your belly and how much he or she needs you.' Abhay gently touched her stomach. 'That reminds me, we should see a doctor tomorrow. Will you apply for leave?'

'Abhay, listen to what I'm saying,' she said sternly. 'I don't want a kid now.'

'You're joking, right?' All the eagerness drained from Abhay's face.

'No, I am not,' she replied, looking straight into his eyes.

Abhay stared back at her, shocked and upset.

• •

Juhi had been very successful in helping her dad grow his farming business with her marketing ideas. She was determined to prove herself because Abhay's taunt that she would not get what she wanted in life still haunted her. But all that she had started in order to divert her attention from Abhay and Pune she had begun to actually enjoy. In fact, she had come up with an exciting idea that she was now discussing with her brother and father.

'Suyash, these days there's a huge demand for organic milk and milk products. I think we should enter the market. We fall under the organic zone and we should take advantage of it. I am sure we can make it big.'

'Juhi, it's not easy to start something new at this age.' Her dad sighed.

'No, that's not true. And we are there with you. Suyash will manage it and I'll do the outfield job to make it reach the market. Trust me, Papa, I really believe we will do well and earn even more. Our profits would multiply and we would be one of the only few who have organic dairy production in the vicinity.'

'And what will happen when you get a good job and leave? How will we manage it then?' her dad asked. 'We are happy with what we are earning now.'

Juhi looked down at her hands—she had no answer to this. What he said did make sense. She wanted to enter the market of organic farming, but was also desperately looking for a job. She was now at a point where she had to decide what she really wanted. Learning about the agro industry and supporting her family had helped her during this difficult time, but did she really want to continue doing this? She started to consider all the probabilities and, after spending three days on it, she made her decision.

'Papa, I am not going to leave. At least not for a job. I want to give my cent percent in setting up an organic dairy farm and not have any regrets later. I'll put my savings into it and will take a loan. Suyash and I will handle it and you continue with the farms.'

'Are you sure about this?' he asked and squeezed her hand. 'I am asking because you always wanted to achieve something in your career. You are saying you don't want to regret not starting this, but I don't want you to wish you had taken a different decision later.'

Juhi smiled. 'Papa, I have made up my mind. Achieving something was my aim, and if it has to come in this way, I don't mind. But Papa, I'll get what I want,' she said firmly.

'You will, beta,' her dad blessed her.

Juhi was excited. She was about to start a new journey, letting go of all the baggage of her past. She had allowed herself to embrace all the possibilities that awaited her. It was her time to embrace change and receive what she had always deserved.

Ten

Three years later

When Juhi had returned home from Pune, she was sailing across a formidable sea with no idea where the wind of destiny would lead her. Her mind was weary and her spirit crushed. She had nearly surrendered to the pain, but had found a way out. She found herself not only wanting to survive but also to work hard towards accomplishing her dream. She realised life had to move in a direction where loving yourself tamed the wild weather of life and all dark emotions could be quashed.

Juhi and Suyash had named their organic dairy 'Happy Cows'. They had both undergone training in organic dairy management and soon they were able to acquire a good market share locally by serving individuals, online stores and bulk orders.

One evening, Suyash suggested, 'Didi, I think we should collaborate with good suppliers now that we are doing well. With an average of two hundred litres of milk production every day, we are getting a profit even after deducting expenses for labour, cow feed, electricity and treatment.'

Juhi nodded. 'In fact, I have a plan to talk with Nature's Basket and other suppliers like that who can buy milk and milk products directly from us. Then we can generate more profits. I was planning to meet their officials sometime this month.'

'I must say your idea of playing melodies for the cows has really worked—milk production was boosted by that. This has worked out so well, Didi; if not for you, we would have never thought of getting into organic dairy farming,' Suyash said. 'Leaving your original career path and settling here must have been difficult for you, I know. Though you never talked about it.'

Juhi thought of the days when she had felt so down, as if there was nothing left in her life. She said, 'You know, I never thought that I would take up the responsibility to grow our family business, and that Maa would allow me to do that. Three years back, when I came here, I was just running away from my life. I had no idea it would turn my life around.'

'I always knew you were a fighter. So what if you didn't get that guy. In search of true love from him, you found yourself. Not many youngsters find strength in their heartbreak. I have friends who were shattered after a break-up and wasted away their life. But you went in a different direction, and I am proud of that.'

'I still think that Maa is not happy. She hasn't talked about my marriage lately, but I can see that she doesn't really want me to do this. Especially because of the losses in the initial days. I told her that this year we have done extremely well, but she didn't react.' Juhi's sadness was visible.

Suyash consoled her saying, 'It's nothing like that. She loves you. When you were in Pune, she worried about you every single day. She just doesn't express it.'

'I hope I make her proud one day.'

'I know you will.' Suyash smiled.

'Don't tell anyone, but I have been working on something else.' Juhi thought it was the right time to tell him. 'I have started writing a book about my life, my love story. It may take time, but I am going to finish it; I won't leave it half way.'

'Are you serious? That's great!' Suyash said, excited to hear that.

'Only Nisha knows, and now you,' Juhi said. Juhi's friendship with Nisha had been unaffected by the distance. They were constantly in touch through calls and messages. Initially, Nisha would pass on updates about Abhay to Juhi on her insistence, but after a year or so, those questions from Juhi had stopped, and even if Nisha mentioned him, it didn't have any impact on Juhi. It had taken some time for Juhi to smile again, but along with her work, her writing had helped her overcome her depression. She didn't allow negative thoughts to consume her, and now was totally free from what she had thought would cage her for her whole life.

'Come, let's go for dinner.' Suyash got up and they headed downstairs.

While they were eating dinner, Juhi and Suyash disclosed their plan to their father. 'Papa, we need to expand the daily capacity as we want to pitch to big guns in the market so our milk can be supplied directly to them,' Juhi said.

'But what if they don't agree? How are we going to manage the expenses then?' her dad said.

'Papa, we need to show them that we are capable of producing as much as the demand is. I will crack the best deal, I am confident about it,' Juhi assured.

But her mom was against it. 'There's no need to put in more money now. We are still recovering what we invested.'

Juhi's dad interrupted. 'Look, I totally agree with what you are saying, but I feel you should approach them first and give a paper plan of our expansion. If we get the deal, we start our preparations instantly. What do you say?'

'Works, Papa.'

Juhi knew that it wasn't going to be cakewalk, but she was up for it. She started working on what her approach would be and the minute details of the plan. She wanted to prove it to herself, more than anyone else, that she could do it. One thing her love story had surely taught her—perseverance.

• •

In the past couple of years, Abhay's life had totally changed. He had levelled up from husband to a father of a two-year-old son, Ameya. Stuti hadn't wanted a baby, but Abhay had managed to convince her. Holding their new-born baby was a feeling that Abhay would never forget. He felt an indescribable love for his son, and had never been more scared in his entire life than the day they strapped their two-day-old into a car seat and drove home. The first few days were scary, but for no reason other than their inexperience. After a few days, it got easier. He had thought fatherhood would be far more stressful and draining than it turned out to be. He figured there'd be way more marital problems, way more drama and way more frustration. However, each and every day with Ameya turned out to be more fun and enjoyable than the last. Of course there were moments when Stuti and Abhay couldn't take the crying and they were constantly exhausted, but every day was a learning experience. Ameya grew up faster than they had expected and they couldn't believe it when he began walking around.

Every day, Abhay would leave Ameya at his parents' house and then go to office. He would pick him up as well, because Stuti's work hours weren't fixed. Abhay had decided to remain at his job as the other offers he'd received gave him a good hike and position but they demanded a lot of his time, and he couldn't afford it as Stuti was very busy.

Abhay had just walked into office when Karan called him to his cabin.

'Abhay, you've been here more than three years and you are one of our best employees. I have a good opportunity for you. The company wants to send three employees from our project to the Singapore office and I am proposing your name for it.'

'Wow, that's really amazing!' Abhay said. He was delighted, but then his face fell thinking about his family. 'But Karan, I have a little baby. I'm not sure if I can leave him and go. Stuti is usually very busy with work and I have to handle him.'

'Don't worry, I know that you cannot leave Ameya alone. The company is allowing family to go along. It's a once-in-a-lifetime opportunity and you shouldn't let it go. Have a word with Stuti and let me know.'

'What would be the duration of our stay there?'

'A couple of years at least,' Karan informed him.

'Okay, thanks. For considering me and thinking that I am capable. I'll let you know in a few days.'

Abhay left the cabin and was about to message Stuti instantly, but then thought he would surprise her after reaching home. He knew she would be happy hearing about this offer and finally he could grab an opportunity. He had sacrificed a lot in the past two years and his professional life had suffered, but no more.

As he walked back to his desk, Nisha noticed his expression and asked, 'Any good news? What did he say?'

'He's proposing my name for the Singapore office. I may have to shift for a couple of years, he said. That experience will be really important for my career ahead.'

'That's amazing! Congratulations,' Nisha said and then asked, 'What about Stuti? Will she be okay about moving to Singapore? I mean, you always said her job is her priority.'

Since Nisha and Abhay had begun to work on the same project, they had become better friends, and Abhay had shared things with her. Abhay thought about it and said, 'That's true, but this time I don't think she'll have a problem because she has a branch office in Singapore.'

'Has she mellowed down now after Ameya?' Nisha asked, and when Abhay was silent, she added, 'I am sorry, I just asked as we haven't spoken about it for quite some time now.'

'No, don't be sorry,' Abhay turned his chair towards her and said. 'You know it all. She hardly gets time from her busy schedule. Sometimes, she's on calls even on weekends, and Ameya is getting naughtier day by day. It's really frustrating.'

Nisha laughed. 'If kids won't be naughty, then who will? You?'

Abhay beamed and said, 'But I am really excited for Singapore. I hope everything goes well and my name gets accepted.'

Nisha congratulated him again and was getting back to work when her phone rang. It was Juhi.

'Hi my darling, how are you?' Nisha asked; she felt good whenever she chatted with Juhi.

'I am good, and I am still waiting for you and Gautam to visit.'

Nisha smiled. 'You know how work life is and—'

Juhi interrupted her. 'I think I'll only have to come there to meet you guys. Listen, I need your help. I remember you telling me that Gautam has a friend who's working at a good position in Hyper City.'

'Yes … Why?'

Nisha listened attentively as Juhi told her the plan she was working on. 'If he can fix a meeting for me with him, that would be great. Maybe sometime next month? I'll be ready with a detailed plan by then.'

'Sure, I'll talk to him. By the way, even I have something to tell you. My parents are meeting Gautam's family to take things ahead. I am keeping my fingers crossed.'

'Fantastic! Give me the good news soon,' Juhi said excitedly and after a brief conversation disconnected the call.

'Was it Juhi?' Abhay asked when Nisha was done with the call.

'Yes, she's really growing each day. I never thought she would shift to organic farming. Now, she is even writing a book.'

'Writing a book? What is it about?' Abhay asked.

Nisha knew but pretended not to. 'I don't know what exactly. But something related to her work,' Nisha lied as she didn't want Abhay to know that he was the central character of the story.

'That's great,' Abhay said. Memories of that night flashed in front of his eyes. 'How silly we were. I hope she isn't still upset about that night and the rubbish I said to her.'

Nisha didn't say anything. She knew it was only that rage and disappointment that Juhi had in her heart for

Abhay that had sparked her determination to be something in life. Sometimes, bad phases help give a direction to your life.

Abhay reached home in the evening after picking up Ameya from his parents' house. Stuti was on her way back too. Once she arrived and had freshened up, she took Ameya in her arms and was playing with him when Abhay disclosed the big news.

'My company is offering to send us to Singapore for a project for around two years. It's a great opportunity for me, and they're allowing family to come along. What do you think? Your company has a branch there so you could have a word with your head and join your Singapore unit, right? Won't it be great?'

Stuti stayed silent and continued to play with Ameya.

'What's the matter? I am telling you something important and you are ignoring me ?' Abhay said, frustrated.

'I heard what you said,' Juhi stated. 'But it isn't feasible. You should turn down the offer.'

Abhay's heart sank. He had truly expected that she would be happy about the offer and readily move with him. But, one again, he felt she didn't care about him or his life.

'What are you saying?' he asked angrily. 'This is a great opportunity for me and you are telling me to just let it go?'

'Yes, I am telling you to let it go. The project I'm in charge of isn't in Singapore. I can't just shift for two years and start from scratch. I have worked really hard to reach where I am today. And everything is going fine, so why do you want to shift? Your parents are taking care of Ameya, your work allows you to spend time with him in the evening, and I am doing my bit, then what's the problem?'

'It's all smooth just for you. I have turned down so many good offers so that I can give time to Ameya. But not you.'

'That's exactly why I didn't want a kid so soon. I told you that, didn't I? But you went on and on and I had to give in. Also, I am not his parent alone. You are his father, and if you are taking care of him, then you aren't doing anyone a favour.'

Abhay shook his head. Earlier, when they fought, he would think that their relationship had changed after marriage. But now he was realising that it had been this way from the very beginning. He sat down, feeling completely without hope, and in an appalled voice expressed what he felt. 'In our relationship, it's only about your dreams, your ambitions, your this and your that. Where do I exist? You'll never understand what I am going through. But I hope you do before it's too late.'

'You are unnecessarily creating drama and I am not up for it. I am tired,' Stuti said and went inside the bedroom.

Abhay picked up Ameya and gazed at him. He was smiling, unaware of what his father was going through.

It seems like everything is off-key these days. You want someone who will give and give but expect nothing in return. It seems as if when we manage to resolve one problem peacefully, we're soon arguing about something else. This bickering has been getting worse over the past year or so. I want to resolve our issues, but you are just into yourself and that hurts me. I always knew that you were career-oriented but never thought that you would turn your passion into obsession, forgetting everything and everyone around you. If one day you notice that we haven't talked for a while or have not gone out to spend some alone time, then you will realise that it's not because I don't care but because you have pushed me away.

• •

The next morning, Abhay woke up to Ameya's cries. Stuti had already left for office. He picked up Ameya and got him ready for the day. Then he placed him in his playpen and got dressed himself. When he came out, Ameya was playing with his toys.

'Hey little man.' Abhay smiled as Ameya rubbed his eyes.

'So, Mama didn't give you breakfast today? Come, I'll give you.' Abhay sat next to Ameya, who was looking around with wide and excited eyes.

Abhay sat Ameya down on his high chair and fed him breakfast. Once done, he looked at the time. He knew Ameya would play for some more time after breakfast, so he put him down on the ground and got ready for office. By the time Abhay was putting on his shoes, every toy in the house had been pulled out.

'That's it Ameya, you are going to Dadi's place.' Abhay got off the couch and picked up Ameya, who started kicking his small limbs. Abhay realised he'd forgotten a file and put him down again to get it from the bedroom. When he came outside, he saw Ameya crying.

'No … no … no Dadi … play,' Ameya said, folding his arms across his chest and stomping his legs. Abhay raised one eyebrow, looking at his son who was giving him attitude.

'No Ameya, I have to go to office now.' Abhay was running late again, but this was nothing new. He wished Stuti would have helped him a bit. He picked up his bag and tried hard not to trip over the toys that were scattered around the living room floor.

'Ameya, have you seen Daddy's car keys?' he called out, but was greeted with silence.

'Ameya, I don't have time to play.' He checked his watch again and groaned when he saw the time.

'Ameya, now,' Abhay said in a stern voice that made the giggling child come out of his hiding spot, keys in his hands. Abhay grabbed them and took him along. He pulled his car out into the morning traffic. Tapping on his steering wheel, Abhay was waiting for the light to change when his phone rang. It was Stuti.

'Have you left?' she asked.

'Yes. It was a messy morning. You should have at least given Abhay breakfast before leaving. He was crying in hunger,' Abhay said, irritated.

'He had only just woken up. And I was getting late. Then I got an urgent phone call and I forgot. He wasn't crying then,' Stuti said.

'How can you forget?'

'I knew you would take care of it.'

'That's not the point,' Abhay continued. 'Anyway I don't want to start the morning on a bad note.' He disconnected the call as the signal changed.

With every passing day, Abhay felt more crushed inside. He would have to tell Karan soon what his decision was about the offer. Also, Stuti's running away from her responsibilities as a mother exasperated him, but there was nothing he could do. Every morning, he hoped things would get better, but nothing ever seemed to change.

Eleven

'Juhi, our parents have agreed and we are getting married next month!' Nisha said excitedly. She had called Juhi to tell her the news as soon as things were fixed.

Juhi had been tallying the accounts when the call came, and now she jumped up from her seat. 'Damn, finally! That's amazing, Nisha. Congratulations.'

'Just congratulations won't work, you have to come and stay here for a few days. We'll celebrate,' Nisha said happily.

'Of course, you don't need to tell me. I would have come even if you hadn't invited me.' Juhi was filled with memories of Pune, the fun times she had spent with Nisha and Gautam. She remembered how they would fight and then pamper each other to calm the other down. Nisha's flirting, Gautam's friendly talks, it all seemed like yesterday.

'I am so happy for both of you,' Juhi said.

'Now I have to spend my entire life with that idiot.' Nisha laughed, and that made Juhi smile too. 'By the way, Gautam had a word with his friend from Hyper City and gave him the brief. Once you finalise the date of your arrival, he'll fix a meeting with him.'

'Fantastic. I'll come at least two days prior so that I can finish the meeting before your wedding,' Juhi said, and then apprehensively asked, 'Is he also coming?'

Nisha didn't understand immediately. 'Who he?'

'Abhay,' Juhi stated. Her voice was quiet as she said his name.

Juhi hadn't talked about him for quite some time now, but Nisha wasn't surprised she was asking. 'I'll invite the entire team, but I'm not sure if he will come. Stuti still decides everything for him.'

After the call, Juhi couldn't get Abhay out of her mind. All of a sudden, she was about to revisit the part of her past that had once completely knocked her down. The only thing that had changed was Juhi wasn't the girl who would run after him to seek love. Or was she?

No, why I am even thinking about him? He doesn't matter to me anymore and whatever is happening in his life, I don't care. The only thing that's scaring me right now is how I will react if I see him at the wedding. Obviously, I won't initiate conversation after how things ended that night, but what if he comes to talk to me with his wife? That would be really awkward. I just hope he doesn't come to the wedding.

Juhi forced herself to stop thinking about Abhay and, for the next one month, she worked hard on the plan that she would present at the meeting that Gautam had scheduled. She was determined to crack the deal.

As decided, she reached Pune two days before Nisha's

wedding. The wedding was going to be in the outskirts of Pune, in Pimpri, where Nisha's parents lived. Nisha had insisted Juhi stay with her at her parents' house, but Juhi decided to book herself into a hotel nearby. On her way to the hotel from Pune airport, she asked the driver to take her past her company offices in Hinjewadi. As they drove down the lanes that once were her daily hang-out spots, she was amazed how every single place brought memories to her mind. Seeing the café at which they'd had mastani, her heartbeat echoed in silence, making her remember how madly in love she had been.

She reached the hotel in the next few minutes and, after she settled down, Nisha and Gautam came to meet her there.

'Juhiiiii ...' Nisha shouted her name as soon as she saw her. 'It's been three long years! I am so fucking happy to see you.'

'You haven't changed a bit,' Juhi commented looking at her. She gave Nisha a hug and told Gautam, 'So, you are finally marrying her. That's sad—you didn't get any other girl in all these years.'

Gautam laughed and said, 'That's true. And now getting hitched for the rest of my life. Poor me.'

'Baby, you have no option now, you have to follow my instructions for your whole life. I am the new boss now,' Nisha said.

'Rest in peace.' Juhi winked and gave him a hug.

'We missed you,' Gautam said.

'Same here. Especially in the initial days when I needed

you both. We were constantly in touch on the phone, but having Nisha by my side always gave me strength.'

'Chuck it, we are not talking about all that,' Nisha said firmly.

'Agreed!' Juhi said. She ordered some snacks for them and said, 'So, what's the plan later?'

'We are going to celebrate tonight! By the way, do you still drink alcohol or is it just milk now.'

'Shut up.' Juhi laughed and punched her lightly.

'What will you drink tonight? Vodka?' Gautam asked.

'Oh hello mister, *we* are going to celebrate. Not you. It's girls' night out tonight.'

'That's ridiculous. I'm coming along. I can't leave you two on your own, especially when you girls plan to get drunk.'

'You go and enjoy with your friends. Don't worry about us,' Nisha said.

'I am not worried about you both, I'm worried about others when you are high,' Gautam said. He then told Juhi, 'By the way, your meeting that was scheduled for tomorrow afternoon has been postponed to a day after our marriage. The guy Rohit said something came up that he couldn't get out of—he said to apologise.'

'Oh shit. I was fully prepped to see him tomorrow.' Juhi's face fell.

'Don't worry, it's confirmed for two o'clock on Monday.'

After spending some time together, Gautam and Nisha left. Juhi had enjoyed herself, reliving past memories with

Nisha. She had not had a drink for three years but had decided to make an exception for tonight. She wanted to celebrate her friend's future properly.

• •

Juhi was ready and waiting for Nisha to arrive. She glanced at herself in the mirror. She was wearing a long skirt and a top, clothes that she rarely wore at home. She was looking forward to the evening—she had missed the fun of night life in Pune. She had cautioned herself that she wouldn't have more than a couple of drinks. The memories of the last time she'd drunk were still trapped in her brain.

'Wow, you look great!' Nisha said when they met. 'Ready for our night of celebration?' she said as they headed out of the hotel. Juhi grinned and nodded.

Nisha had decided that they would go to Tripping Club. Once there, they ordered drinks.

'Cheers to my last night as a bachelorette. Though I am sure we will have many more such evenings even in the future, after locking my husband in the bedroom.'

'Cheers to a sexy and rocking married life,' Juhi said, raising her glass. 'I still can't believe you are getting married. Now my mother's discussions about my marriage will restart once I get back home.'

'I am surprised that she has allowed you to remain single till now.' Nisha giggled and took a sip of her vodka. 'You staying in your parents' house without getting married is an achievement in itself. Must be much more difficult than spending fifteen weeks in *Big Boss*. Isn't it?'

'Totally. But I got so busy in my work, I don't know how three years went by.'

'Seriously, I also feel the same way. Like it's only been a few days since we were staying together. Once you left, I felt all alone. I mean, Gautam was always there, but a boyfriend can never take a friend's place.'

Juhi laughed, she couldn't agree more. Juhi ordered another drink and asked Nisha, 'So, are you going to stay healthy even after marriage?'

'Healthy? What do you mean? Have I gained weight?' Nisha stood up so that Juhi could check her properly.

'Flirting keeps you healthy was your mantra. So does that continue?' Juhi said laughing.

'Oh that...' Nisha laughed and said, 'If Gautam doesn't have a problem, why would I stop? It totally depends on him.'

'You guys are really cute.'

'That I agree. But it's Gautam who has handled me pretty well. I mean, I don't need to tell you that, you know it all. But there was not a single day after you went when he made me feel bad or unimportant. He always took care of the small things that I tend to forget and it amazes me how he could figure out the sadness behind my smiles.'

'I agree, he is a sweetheart and you are lucky to have him,' Juhi said. The French fries they had ordered were placed on the table.

'I always wonder what I did to deserve him. I guess the gods must have been pleased with me,' Nisha said.

Juhi smiled, and went silent. Nisha noticed her discomfort and asked, 'What happened all of a sudden?'

Juhi wasn't sure if she should say what was going on in her mind, but she did. 'Look, I don't know if I should ask you this but I'm unable to keep it to myself.'

'What?' Nisha was confused.

'Is Abhay coming, did he say anything?' Juhi couldn't look into her eyes.

'It's the second time you're asking, Juhi. Do you want him to come?'

Juhi instantly said, 'No, no … in fact, I don't want him to come. It's over from my side. Just that …'

'Chill, I was joking,' Nisha interrupted. 'Like I told you, I really don't know if he is coming or not. Most decisions in his life are taken by Stuti, and would she be okay coming? I don't know.'

'Why doesn't he stand up for himself?' Juhi asked. *I don't want to even know, why am I asking,* Juhi asked herself. *I really don't care.*

Nisha told Juhi whatever she knew about the last couple of years—how he had not been able to fulfil his desires. She said, 'He just want to escape the struggles, but he hasn't been able to.'

Hearing this, Juhi felt bad. 'I always felt he always deserved better.'

'Anyway, why are we discussing him? It's my bachelorette.' Nisha raised her glass again.

Her favourite song, *Shape of You*, started playing, and Nisha jumped up to dance.

When the song got over, Nisha returned. 'Back already?' Juhi asked.

'Because you are not joining me on the dance floor. Come along.'

'No way. You know I don't dance.,' Juhi said.

'Come on, we never know when we will able to do all of this again. I am getting married; you'll get married one day, and then life will be boring.'

The thought of marriage reminded her of Abhay. She accompanied Nisha onto the dance floor, but her mind went back to those old days. She had believed she had moved on. She had convinced her heart that she had no feelings for Abhay. She had thought it was over, but was it really?

• •

'Stuti, you'll get dressed soon?' Abhay asked as he ironed the shirt he planned to wear for the wedding.

Stuti was sitting with Ameya in the living room. 'No … you go, I'll handle Ameya.'

'Handle Ameya?' Abhay kept the iron aside and walked into the living room. 'What do you mean? All three of us are going together.'

'And who decided that? You alone?' Stuti said. 'I get just one day at home and most of the time I am on call even on Sundays. Today, I don't want to go out anywhere. Please.'

'It's the first marriage we will be attending after ours. And it doesn't look good. All my colleagues will be there, what am I going to tell them as to why my wife didn't come along?' Abhay said, agitated.

'I don't even know anyone there, what am I supposed to do?' Stuti said.

'What are we supposed to do at weddings? Just wish the couple and come back. That's it. Before marriage you even came to my office party once, and now you don't want to attend a marriage. Crazy.' Abhay sighed.

'Please, Abhay. Spare me for a day.'

'Spare you for a day? On weekdays it's your office time, on Sunday it's your me time. Where's *our* time? I sometimes feel that I should just disappear somewhere without telling anyone. I am fed up.'

'Why do you have to crib each and every time? We are not living a college love story here that we have to forget our careers and just romance in a park. We have to run the house. We have responsibilities.'

Abhay walked away, tired of arguing with her. He couldn't figure out how and when their love for each other had started fading. There was a time they had both loved each other, but something had happened, and they had drifted apart so much that it was slowly burning his heart into ashes.

••

'How am I looking?' Nisha asked Juhi.

'Nisha, this is the fifth time you are asking.' Juhi held her shoulders. She could see the panic on her face. 'You are looking gorgeous. Trust me, Gautam is going to fall for you all over again when he sees you in this outfit.'

Nisha blushed. 'I am just nervous. I am excited but the anxiety is also terrible.'

'Beta, I know what you are thinking.' Nisha's mother held her hand. 'You will be a good daughter-in-law. All these years you have made our house so happy with your presence, and I know you will continue doing that in your new house too. And never think that this isn't your house just because you are married.'

Nisha noticed a teardrop on her mother's cheeks. She gripped her hand tightly and they just looked at each other. They stayed like that for some time and then she let go of Nisha's hand, brushed her cheeks, smiled and said, 'Come, beta, the rituals are going to begin in the next few minutes.'

When Nisha was on the stage, Juhi went to greet her former colleagues.

'How's your Happy Cows business coming along?' Karan asked. 'I read about it in an online magazine that had interviewed you. "The girl who left her job and founded an organic milk company". I must say, you were brilliant in the interview.'

'Thanks.' Juhi smiled and turned her gaze to Arpit. 'What's up with you?'

'All good. I'm getting married in the next few months,' Arpit disclosed.

'Oh wow, that's great.' Juhi congratulated him.

The next moment, they could see a flash of discomfort on her face and Karan asked, 'What happened?'

'Nothing, I just remembered I have to keep Nisha's mangalsutra ready.' She excused herself and left. But that was not the truth. She had seen Abhay walk into the wedding hall and she wanted to escape. Juhi had seen him after such a long time. She felt the adrenaline rush through her when she saw him smiling and laughing with Karan and the others. Just then Nisha's mother asked her to bring the mangalsutra and garlands, and she left the room, thinking, *Abhay, you have changed. You look ten years older than your age. I can see sadness in those eyes and distress in that face behind that smile. I thought it would disturb me to see you after so many years. But I am fine. I am not sure what it is, but I certainly don't feel like running away. Before you arrived, I hoped I would not have to face you today. And after seeing you, my first instinct was to avoid you, but then when I looked at you, I realised I am no longer that old Juhi. Maybe I am feeling bad for you, or maybe I still have feelings for you?*

Juhi handed over the things Nisha's mom had asked for and came down from the stage. She was walking towards the food counter to check if everything was in place when she saw Abhay in front of her. For a moment, she was speechless; she had not expected Abhay to make the first move. She looked at him, trying to gauge what he was thinking. More than that, she was trying to see what her feelings were.

'How are you?' he asked clumsily.

'I am good, what about you?' Nisha replied, uneasiness evident in their body language.

'Yes, even I am fine.'

After a second's silence, Abhay continued. 'So, for how many days are you here?'

'Just a few more days. I have some work here,' Juhi said.

'How do you feel coming back to Pune after so many years? Has the city changed?'

'Not really. But people have. Look at you.'

Abhay thought she was aware of what he was going through. Juhi saw that his face had turned thoughtful and said, 'Don't take it seriously, I meant look at the white hair in your beard. Too stressed about work, it seems.'

'Oh ya …' Abhay sighed. 'Life's got tougher.'

'Ya, I can understand, you are a married man now.' She smiled and added, 'Anyway, how's your married life going on? How's Stuti?'

'All good,' Abhay lied. He felt like opening up his heart to her; somehow, he felt she would be able to help. *Should I tell her? Will she understand me and have a neutral perspective?* Fear stopped him from doing so and he changed the topic. 'Nisha told me that you are writing a book. Is that true?'

'Yes, but I am not getting the right ending.' Juhi was surprised he had remembered what Nisha had told him. 'I can't think of a perfect climax.'

There was an awkward silence between them. Abhay gave her an apologetic look and said, 'I am sorry for what happened between us.'

'Leave it. No hard feelings,' Juhi said, acting as if it had not affected her.

Abhay still wanted to pour his heart out to her. Somewhere he felt she wouldn't be judgemental and would give an honest opinion of the situation. 'How about a coffee tomorrow? Or a mastani that you loved?'

The flashback of that first date played in her mind. Juhi didn't say yes, but she didn't say no either.

Would Juhi accept his proposal? Did she really want to go out and spend time with him knowing he was no more a priority to her? Or was he? Juhi had not imagined that their paths would cross again. But it had happened, and neither of them knew what repercussions it would bring.

Twelve

'Hi Nisha …' Juhi said in a mischievous tone. 'How was your night?'

'Too tiring, nothing happened. We were so fucked up standing like mannequins, clicking pictures with guests, that we crashed as soon as we were in our room.'

Juhi laughed. 'Poor guys. Anyway, I am leaving for the meeting. Can you tell Gautam to send me Rohit's number?'

'Ya, sure.' Gautam was in front of her and Nisha conveyed Juhi's message. 'He is sending it right away,' Nisha said.

Juhi paused and then, taking a deep breath, said, 'I met Abhay yesterday. He wants to meet me.'

Nisha was taken aback. 'So, what did you say?'

'Nothing. And I haven't thought about what to do yet. I am focusing on my meeting. But he looked upset, as if he wanted to tell me something. I am not sure.'

'Think about it later, Juhi,' Nisha advised her. 'All the best for your meeting.'

'Thanks.'

Juhi hung up and left for her meeting. On the way, thoughts of whether or not to meet Abhay made her restless but she consciously tried to push them away. She needed to focus on her presentation.

She had already mailed Rohit a brief on how Happy Cows operated and the kind of deal she was looking for. Juhi skimmed through the file she had prepared and checked the PPT once again. When she reached the café where the meeting was to take place, she called Rohit to ask his whereabouts. He had just parked his car, he said, and would be there in a minute.

When Juhi saw Rohit, she realised it was the same friend she had met in the club with Gautam.

'Hi Rohit, how are you doing?' She got up from her chair and shook hands with him.

'Nice meeting you again. I hope you remember we had met once? I had tagged along with Gautam.'

'Of course. But you have got fitter now. What's the secret?' Juhi asked, recollecting he was quite hefty back then.

'Yoga helps you stay fit and reduces work stress,' Rohit replied with a smile.

Juhi smiled and then asked, 'I hope you got the time to go through the mail.'

'I did. I went through your brief, and I must say, it's impressive.'

They ordered sandwiches and then Juhi discussed her plan with him in more detail.

'As you know, seventy per cent of the milk sold in India is adulterated. But Happy Cows guarantees purity.

Milk only comes from our own dairy farm and undergoes stringent quality checks. Currently we are selling at many locations in Madhya Pradesh within a limited radius, as it has to be served fresh. I want to collaborate with your brand so we can make it available in all the stores in Bhopal and nearby cities.'

'I checked that it's FSSAI certified too, but I have to talk with officials. You can consider this an informal meet. Don't worry, I'll represent you to the decision-makers as Gautam is a dear friend of mine. But we have around twenty stores in the vicinity where you can sell. Do you think you can fulfil the demand if things work out?'

'I know that currently we don't have that daily capacity but once we have a deal, that's the first thing we are going to do and only then would we come on board. We are okay with the share that your brand wants to keep as per policy, but there will be no middlemen. We plan to arrange the delivery ourselves.'

Juhi and Rohit discussed a few more legalities and terms and concluded the meeting.

'Leave it to me. I'll get back to you in a few days,' Rohit assured her. 'I hope you will be around in Pune?'

'Of course. I'll wait for you to get in touch.'

They were about to leave when Juhi's phone beeped. It was a text message from Abhay.

'Are we meeting today? If we are, then I will leave office accordingly.'

Juhi said bye to Rohit, and then contemplated what she should reply to Abhay. She was nervous she would again develop feelings for him and she didn't want to get into any mess again now that he was married. She decided to ignore his text and carried on with other meetings she had scheduled with a few investment firms. But no matter how much she tried to distract herself, a part of her wanted to meet him. She couldn't understand herself what was tempting her to do so.

A day later, Abhay texted her again. 'I'm still waiting for your answer. If you don't want to meet me, you can tell me directly. I won't feel bad. You don't need to ignore me.'

Juhi stared at the message.

Why do I want to meet you? I know that I have moved on, yet in some corner of my heart, I feel we should talk. Maybe I want to know for sure whether or not I still have feelings for you. I want to know if your presence still has the same impact on me. I think, before going back home, I want to let go of all the baggage of the past. I don't want it to haunt me and for that, we need to meet once. Then, I can walk forward in life without looking back even once!

So Juhi replied, 'Let's meet. The same mastani café.'

Juhi had finally decided to meet Abhay with the intention of freeing herself from her past. But was it a wise decision? Or was she allowing the demons to enter and rout her soul completely?

• •

Juhi reached the café and texted Abhay. He replied that he was on his way.

Juhi still remembered the table at which she and Abhay had sat the first time they'd come here. She had been nervous to visit the café because of the memories attached to it. In a fragmented mind space, memories can be violent winds. It wasn't just memories of him, but memories of herself, those reminders of the many pains she had gone through. The only thing that could hurt her more than her love for Abhay was the pain of the memories of the person she had been, the things she once had done—the person she would never want to be again. Her mind was occupied with those thoughts when Abhay arrived. They greeted each other and Abhay sat across from her.

'I thought you would not meet me,' he said and smiled.

Juhi wondered what to say. She shrugged and said, 'I was just occupied with a few work-related things. I didn't get any time to reply.'

Abhay played with the menu card. Finally, he looked up at her apprehensively and then again looked down when he spoke. 'I've always thought that it shouldn't have ended the way it did.'

'I told you, it's fine.' Juhi sat up straight on her chair.

'I know it wasn't fine because you left your job. And I felt guilty for shouting at you like that in front of Stuti. I shouldn't have.'

'Actually, that made me find my true self.' Juhi was aware that if that hadn't happened, she would have still been working in the same company and would have never ended up doing what she really wanted.

'I really enjoyed working with the team that was around when I joined. Many have switched jobs, and now it's Nisha and me together all the time, with the rest giving cold vibes.' Abhay laughed.

Abhay continued to narrate stories about office.

I used to look at you differently when you would go on talking. I used to love getting lost in your eyes. My heart used to beat faster and my legs used to tremble. You know, the feelings you get when in love. But now I don't feel the same. I think my thoughts are getting clearer now.

'You haven't changed a bit.' Abhay snapped his fingers in front of her eyes and beamed. 'You again activated your mute mode.'

'Oh no, I was just thinking about something,' Juhi covered up.

'How's your business going?' Abhay asked.

'Going good. We have plans to expand in the coming months.' Juhi crossed her fingers and smiled. 'So, how's your married life going? Nisha told me you have a kid?'

'Yes, Ameya.' Abhay showed her a picture on his mobile phone. 'He is too naughty.'

'I am sure. He is cute.' Juhi looked at the picture and handed the phone back to Abhay.

I should have got jealous seeing your kid. But I am not. I don't feel the same anymore, Juhi said to herself.

It seemed like Abhay was going around in circles and not actually saying what he wanted to. Juhi could sense it. After meeting so many people for work, she could gauge what was going in the other person's mind.

'I don't think you asked me here for a casual conversation, Abhay,' she said finally.

'Actually … it's nothing like that.' Abhay coughed at the straightforward statement. 'I mean I just wanted to meet; it's been a long time, right?'

'You can talk about anything with me, if you want.'

That's why I am here, Abhay said in his mind and leaned forward to speak. His phone rang. It was Stuti. He disconnected the call and tried to smile at Juhi. Stuti called again, but once again he rejected the call. Juhi frowned, confused by his odd behaviour.

'I don't know if I should say this, but I feel something's wrong,' Juhi said. She wasn't sure Abhay would like her directness, but seeing no objection from his side and a thoughtful look from him, she continued. 'If you feel that something is stopping you from revealing what's in your heart, then just get over it. The more you keep your feelings caged inside you, the more you will feel trapped. I have gone through it and I know how it feels. Don't be nervous about what I'm going to think or whoever you are speaking to. People may judge you, but it's your life finally.'

Abhay remained quiet. *I know what you are saying is right. But should I really tell you what's going on? I don't want to be misunderstood. People don't easily believe that even men can feel trapped and helpless in a situation. We are judged even before we explain our side of things. I feel that if I say something, I would have to explain it over and over again and that is exhausting, especially when the outcome would be the same.*

Abhay was pulled back from his thoughts when the waiter placed their orders on the table. The mango mastani that they loved.

'It seems that you have activated your mute mode.' Juhi laughed.

Abhay laughed too and told her to finish the mastani in one go, and the next instant he started gulping it down. Juhi watched him drink and attempted the same but couldn't do it. She didn't force herself, as she didn't feel the need to impress him anymore. After having their mastani, Juhi said she needed to leave.

She felt she had relieved an emotional burden she had carried all these years. She walked away feeling much more at peace.

I was right, I don't feel the same anymore. You no longer have control over my feelings. It makes me so happy. I loved you, I really did, Abhay. There's no way I can prove it, only my heart knows how much I did. But today, I have moved on completely. I always thought that the abrupt end to our relation would disturb me my whole life and I kept running away from my past, but not anymore. You'll always have that special place in my heart, Abhay, but now I know you are just my past. Also, thank you, Abhay, for giving me the end to my story.

••

Abhay left the café but didn't go home. He wandered on the streets alone, knowing that he had to take some decisions about his marriage and his life. He had made up his mind that he couldn't continue like this, he was tired of hoping for a change in Stuti's attitude. He also had to inform Karan about his decision on Singapore in the next four days. Stuti had not changed her mind, but he was unable to refuse the offer. He was tired of feeling like a failure. He felt empty and depressed.

This hurts. I remember the good times and the love we shared. Last night, I cried for an hour as I thumbed through our photo album and relived our wedding. But you didn't even bother to see what I was doing. You aren't the same Stuti that I loved. It feels like I am giving everything to someone who just doesn't care. Our son will soon celebrate his third birthday. And you don't seem to care about him either. When did you turn that selfish? Or were you always this way and I couldn't see it? What have I done to deserve this? I have reached a point where holding on to an invisible thread has become ridiculous. I have no one to speak to. I know that even if I do, I will be told to understand. That's what happens most of the time in our society. And our families are no different. The bad times are beginning to outnumber the good and that's starting to affect my outlook on life. We use up all our energy bickering and then resolving things, and these days we don't even find a resolution, we just walk away. If there were just one difficult subject, we could learn to avoid it. But we tend to move from one issue to another, quarrelling about anything and everything—which has brought me to a hard decision. I can't live like this anymore.

It was almost midnight and Abhay still hadn't reached home. He was drinking in a bar alone, frustrated. Stuti had called him multiple times, as had his colleagues. He didn't answer their calls either as he knew Stuti must have informed them that he was not home yet. Eventually, when she started calling continuously, he picked up.

'Do you know, the number of times you called today is far more than you have in the past entire year,' Abhay said sarcastically.

'Where the fuck are you? I have been calling you since evening! Who are you roaming with?

'I don't owe you any explanations,' Abhay said. 'The fact is, I am fed up of pretending that I am happy with you and that everything is fine between us.'

'Stop talking nonsense and come home,' Stuti said loudly.

'I am not coming back. Ever. And this isn't any nonsense. You are so blind, you don't see the pain I am going through. I go to work irritable after our daily fight at breakfast and am soon snapping at my co-workers. I don't look forward to coming home anymore either, and try and find extra work to do at my desk. Our entire lives have just been about you and your dreams, your growth, your career. That's it.'

'Have you lost your mind?' Stuti yelled. 'You are planning to leave me just because you are jealous of my achievements? Don't blame me for the failure of your career. You are behind others not because of me, but because of yourself.'

Abhay felt he had been stabbed by her words.

'That's your problem. You don't realise what you say when you are annoyed. I sometimes don't understand if this egoistic side is your real face or the easy-going one you show when you are in normal mood.'

'Don't try to blame it on me for no good reason.

Check your phone—how many times I have called and how many unread messages you have received.'

'Stuti, trying to improve this relationship is all I've focused on lately, and it has negatively impacted other areas of my life—my job, my friends, my relationship with my parents. Today I met Juhi and I was not even able to tell her what I am going through. That's when I realised what have I done to myself. I have been stressed out and on edge with everyone around me. I need to focus on getting back to feeling happy and at peace with myself and my life,' Abhay said and disconnected the call.

He walked out of the bar and went up to his car. He opened the door and got inside when he felt someone sitting in the front passenger seat. He was terrified and almost got outside again in fear, but then when he looked properly, he saw himself. His conscious self. He felt he was drunk and hallucinating, but his conscious self broke the silence.

'You are not hallucinating. It's me, your real self.'

'What do you want?'

'I want you to stop being the way you are. I want you to realise your worth. If something is stopping you, get over it. The more you keep your feelings caged inside you, the more you will feel trapped,' it stated.

'But that's not you. Juhi told me this in the evening,' Abhay recollected.

'So, what was wrong in what she said? You are not happy in this relationship, it has turned toxic for you. You have to end it if you want to regain your life and happiness. You have tried enough to change the situation, but you know that it's not going to. Then why are you lying to yourself? And till when will you run away from the truth? It happens—sometimes relationships don't go as planned. You need to realise when to end things. And you are already too late.'

'But we have a son. What is his fault?' Abhay said.

'Nothing. But what's yours? He will understand as he grows up that you are just ending your relationship with Stuti and not with him. You'll always be his father. But ask yourself, do you always want to be Stuti's husband?'

Abhay thought for a moment and the next instant he saw no one. He looked around in confusion, but the incident cleared his mind. He would choose his life, his happiness and the dreams that he had buried deep inside. He had finally taken a decision to start a new life.

Thirteen

Life isn't just about taking chances, it's also about giving yourself a chance to bring about a change. Abhay and Juhi were embarking on a new beginning, giving themselves a chance to change the journey of their lives.

Juhi had got a call from Rohit in the morning, asking to meet. Juhi was anxious to know what the team had said, but he insisted on meeting and that made her nervous. She reached the same café where they had met previously. Rohit was already waiting for her. After greeting each other, Juhi came straight to the point, unable to hold back anymore.

'What did they say? Positive or negative?' Juhi asked, rubbing her hands and moving back and forth on her chair.

Rohit laughed. 'Oh God, you look so tense. You should relax,' he said. 'Okay, so I did put forth your proposal as you know and after our Zoom call with them yesterday, they have come to a conclusion. They are ready to take it forward and have accepted your deal.' He had a wide smile on his face.

'Oh wow, seriously?' Juhi almost jumped out of her chair.

'Yes, but like you mentioned, you have to ramp up your production as soon as possible. In the beginning, the purchase order would be for our twelve main stores that are in your delivery reach. After evaluating the response for two weeks, we plan to make it available in all twenty stores. Which means the supply should be approximately five hundred litres.' He folded his arms over his chest. 'So get ready to work round the clock.'

Juhi smiled. 'I'm looking forward to it. Thank you so much.'

Rohit smiled back and said, 'Oh come on, you deserved it. Your plan was excellent. All the very best. I am sure with your dedication, even our region will soon get your products.'

Juhi couldn't believe she had actually cracked the deal. It was a dream moment for her. She had always believed in herself and her plan, but believing and executing it are two different things and she had enacted on her belief.

Rohit leaned forward, 'So, shall we celebrate with a glass of wine?'

'Oh ya, sure. Why not.'

Over the next half an hour, Juhi listened to Rohit's suggestions, trying to absorb lessons from his years of experience. When he left, she called her father to inform him. She had never been so excited to tell him something. It was he who had supported her throughout, and she wanted to break the news to him first.

'Papa—there's good news!' she said as soon he answered the call.

'What happened?'

'We got the deal!' she said happily. 'Now it's time to take a leap and taste success. We have to increase our daily limit to one thousand litres.' Juhi repeated what Rohit had told her.

In an emotional voice, her father said, 'You did it, beta ... you did it. I am so happy for you.' He took a deep breath and wiped his tears. 'Now, when are you coming back?'

'In a couple of days. I have had meetings with a couple of investment firms here, so once I update them about the deal, I'll be back. Till then, ask Suyash to have a word with those firms with whom we have had discussions before. He'll know what I mean.'

After she hung up, Juhi called Nisha and shared the news with her. She thanked Gautam for his help. Both were delighted and promised to visit her farm once they were back from their honeymoon.

Juhi's flight had taken off but Abhay's world was crashing down.

• •

Abhay reached home in the early hours of the morning and saw that the bedroom door was locked. He wanted to tell Stuti right then and there that he didn't want to continue their relationship. He knocked on the door for a few minutes and even called out her name, but Stuti didn't respond. He eventually slept in the living room, deciding to talk to her when she got up in the morning.

When he woke up and checked the time, he saw it was already noon and thought he had missed his chance as Stuti must have already left for office. He walked into the bedroom to see Stuti sitting with Ameya, trying to make him take his nap.

He could see from Stuti's face that she was furious. 'I want to talk to you, please come outside. I don't want to disturb Ameya,' Abhay said.

Stuti walked into the living room behind Abhay and sat on the sofa. 'Now you will give all the explanations for coming late, but it's of no use. You already told me yesterday that you don't owe me any explanation.'

Abhay closed his eyes and leaned his head back in disgust. 'What's the use of explaining when you won't even understand. I want to tell you that I can't live with you anymore. You are so different from what you were before. You take no notice of how I feel, what I'm going through. When you told me to turn down the Singapore offer, that was the last straw.'

'Oh, so it's all because of that offer? How can you be so immature?' Stuti said angrily.

'What if you had got the same offer? I am sure you wouldn't have even consulted me before accepting it. But that is not the point. Even now, you feel there's nothing wrong in living like this.' Abhay sighed, he got up from his chair and walked towards the window. He looked outside, recalling their dating days. 'I will never forget the beauty I saw when I first set eyes on you. I was never tired of praising you. You made me promises that we would be each other's happiness and I never imagined you wouldn't keep it. Life was exciting, we enjoyed nights out, exotic holidays, I felt loved and wanted. We got married and had a child. Then everything changed. I soon realised that I wasn't your priority and never would be. I often want to scream, where is the girl I fell in love with?'

Stuti didn't react to what he had said. She simply told him, 'I know why you are doing all this. And I will not let you do it. If you think you can just leave me and walk away from this marriage, then you are mistaken.'

'But why do you want me in your life? You don't need me. We never talk, we never spend time together, we rarely eat together and I don't even remember the last time we went out on a holiday. It's better we just part ways,' Abhay said with a heavy heart.

The doorbell rang. Abhay was surprised; he didn't know who it could be at this time. Stuti got up and walked towards the door. 'Why don't you tell all the things you told me to your parents. They are here. It would be better, I guess. I'm sure they would love to hear what their son desires.'

Abhay was shocked.

'Why did you call them? This is between the two of us,' Abhay said.

Stuti didn't respond and opened the door. His parents had overheard what he'd said.

'It's good that she told us. Else we don't know what all you would have done,' Abhay's mother said. She looked upset. Even his father looked unhappy.

'What has she told you? What are you saying?' Abhay asked his mother, baffled.

'The truth. Are you going to confess everything to us and explain what made you do it?' his father said.

'What are you talking about?' Abhay was still confused.

'Don't pretend as if you don't know anything. Where were you the whole night? You were with that girl, right? What's her name ...?' his mother said.

'Juhi ...' his father said. 'Stuti told us that you met her yesterday and then didn't come home the entire night and even called to say you want to break this marriage.'

'What nonsense!' Abhay got up, furious, and looked at Stuti. She stood with her head down, like she was distressed after finding out about her husband's affair. Abhay looked at his parents and said, 'If that is what Stuti told you, then it's a lie.'

Abhay disclosed the truth to them and told them what he had gone through in the past few months, but his parents were unmoved.

'If you even think of ending this marriage, we are dead for you. You may have forgotten that we have relatives and close ones to whom we are answerable, but we haven't. And, think about Ameya. You both sort this out on your own,' his mother said.

'You are a man. You should be the one who should take care of the family and act responsibly. Not the other way round.'

That was not the end. After they left, Stuti's father called him and warned him not to leave his daughter. 'I'll file a case against you for harassing my daughter, Abhay. Don't act like a coward and run away from your marriage. Be responsible.'

After he had disconnected his father-in-law's call, Abhay collapsed on the sofa. 'This is ridiculous. I never thought that you would stoop to such a level. Was playing this victim card necessary? You are at fault and they're all pointing fingers at me. Wow.'

'I just told them that you hadn't come home and when they asked with whom you were, I had to tell them. I never told your parents that you are having an extramarital affair. And neither did I tell mine that. They just assumed it. And anyway, that doesn't justify your actions,' Stuti retaliated.

'I was already dejected and thank you for making me feel more miserable. Congratulations. You win, I lose.'

It was an earthshattering thing for Abhay. He felt like he had lost the courage to fight and had no strength anymore; like he would have to suffer for the rest of his life.

How easily we blame someone without knowing the real story behind it. Forget some absolute stranger, how easily even my parents pointed fingers at me; they have known me my entire life and still didn't believe what I said. Isn't it strange? I had finally summoned up the strength to walk out of this mess. Now, I can see no way forward. Whichever way I turn, I find a road block.

• •

Juhi met with the investment firms with whom her talks were on, but they finally rejected the proposal. Juhi was upset because, after cracking the deal, she had assumed that they would readily accept it. She called Suyash to find out what the decision was of the firms they had met in Bhopal.

'Any luck there? Because I didn't get a thumbs-up here,' she said.

'Didi, it's almost done here,' Suyash said. He had just met with the firm officials in the morning. 'I have updated them that we have acceptance from a brand for our products. They just want to see that official mail and then we are done.'

'Amazing! That means we'll get at least half the amount of what we have to put in,' Juhi said.

'Yes. Everything is going as per plan. Don't stress,' Suyash said.

Juhi hung up feeling a bit relieved and ordered in-room dining in her hotel. She switched on the television and was browsing channels when she got a call from Nisha.

'Have you come back from your honeymoon?' she asked when she picked up the call.

'It was a short trip. Gautam had some prior commitments. We came yesterday early morning itself,' Nisha told her.

'What? Why didn't you tell me? I am still in Pune.'

'Oh! I thought you had left already.'

'Idiot.'

Nisha took a deep breath and then said, 'Actually. I called you to ask you to have a word with Abhay. If you're still in Pune, maybe you can meet him once. He is really in bad shape.'

'Why, what happened?' Juhi asked.

Nisha repeated what Abhay had told her and said, 'The last time you met him, he felt he should have talked. But he was afraid. I'm sure if you meet him again, he will speak, and you never know, maybe it will help him find the right direction.'

'Did he tell you that he wants to meet me?' Juhi asked.

'No. Somehow, I feel you understand him and I know you don't have feelings for him anymore. He is in trouble. If you can manage to meet once before you leave ...' Nisha said.

'Okay, I'll message him.'

She texted Abhay, 'I am going back tomorrow. Want to meet today? You can give me the farewell that you couldn't give last time.'

Abhay was in the office when he received her message. When he read it, he felt nervous to meet after all that had happened, but he finally decided that his situation couldn't get worse than it was, so he agreed. This time, he would tell her everything, he thought.

Juhi saw Abhay walking in and when he joined her at the table, she could immediately sense he was tormented and even more miserable than before. Her heart ached looking at his face; he was quiet and dull, as if after fighting a fierce storm he had given up and was drowning.

'What's the matter? You are in bad shape. Is everything okay?' Juhi asked. She did not want to reveal that Nisha had told her everything. She wanted to leave it up to Abhay to discuss the matter or not.

'No, I'm not really okay,' Abhay said, looking dejected. 'Everything is a mess.'

'What happened? You can tell me.' Juhi said, a concerned look in her eyes. Abhay saw that and shook his head, remembering how helpless he had felt in the last twenty-four hours.

Juhi held his hand to comfort him and asked him to speak up.

Abhay took a deep breath and said, 'I don't want to continue with Stuti. I can see now that our relationship was always toxic and she was always self-centred. I was just blind to it. When I first began to see these traits, I felt that things would change, but it's just getting worse, day by day. Initially, I restrained myself from saying anything to people because we had been in a relationship before marriage, and I thought I would look like a fool if I say I am not happy now. Obviously, people believe that if you have had a love marriage, compatibility is the last thing you should be worried about. But of late, I can't even bear to be around her.'

He continued to tell her everything in detail and Juhi listened carefully.

When he was done, she asked, 'Did you tell Stuti or your parents exactly how you feel? I mean, I am sure you would have told her how she is at fault and what it is that she's doing that is wrong, but did you tell her it's because of her actions that you are getting affected?'

'Yes, I have told her. I even told her many times how our relationship is being affected because of all this. I am not saying it's only her fault, even I am to be blamed for not conveying it to her before it was too late. I turned a blind eye and covered up for her and that has backfired. No one believes me, not even my parents ... Do you at least believe me?' Abhay asked, looking at her with hope. Juhi looked back at him, seeing clearly the trauma he had had to endure silently.

Three years back she had loved him and he had loved someone else. They parted ways to live their own journeys and today both had reached extreme ends. She was thriving, while he was fighting for survival.

Fourteen

How strange is life! When tough times come, a few evolve and their true potential is unleashed, but a few succumb to the grief and forget what they are capable of. They lose their identity. But life is about evolving and not resisting change.

In the café, Abhay was waiting to hear Juhi's response. She took her own time and then expressed her view. 'See Abhay, I am no one to tell you what you should do. But once we were friends and, because of that, I have a strong suggestion—don't waste any more time standing on the shore watching your life flow past. If you really think that you have given it all that you can but it's still not working, then you have to take a tough call.'

Abhay eyes filled with tears hearing that. 'I am glad at least you believe me. I thought, like the others, you would also just—'

Juhi didn't let him complete. 'I know one thing, and that is you cannot lie. I have seen that; you were always honest in your relationship even when—' Juhi paused all of a sudden. She wanted to refer to the time when she had loved him madly and he never took advantage of it. But she controlled herself and continued, 'I am not sure if I should say it, but even then, we always felt that you deserved better.'

Abhay shook his head. 'She did love me very much. We had dreams together. I just never realised when our dreams turned into only her dreams. I am suffocating.'

'I can understand. Perhaps you can't bear the impact that your decision will have on your son and family. Perhaps you don't want to hurt anyone. Perhaps you can't afford it? Perhaps you're scared. Perhaps there are a million reasons to stay and only one to leave. Your happiness. Maybe you've done as much as you can for as long as you can, and now it's simply time.'

'Do you think it's right to do so?'

'Sometimes it's not about choosing between right and wrong, but choosing the better of the wrong choices.' Juhi had a slight smile on her face.

'But what will people say?' Abhay said.

'Do you just want to continue with a fake smile for the sake of people? Caring about what others are saying is like giving them the opportunity to control your breath. And you cannot do that. People will always judge but you cannot let that affect you or your decisions; this is something you will face literally everywhere. If I had gone by what people say, I would have been in grief all my life. I wouldn't have opted for a job in Pune, I would have been married by now and would have never dared to start Happy Cows and would have never dared to even confess how I feel to you, knowing you had a girlfriend.' Juhi hadn't intended to bring up the past, but she couldn't take back her words now. In any case, she felt what she said was the truth.

Juhi continued after a brief silence, 'Anyway, it's not about me, it's about you. What I mean is, once you start ignoring these voices and push yourself to do what you think is right for you, it will give you confidence and these noises in your head will fade away. It's time to stop pretending and time to face up to the truth, scary as that is.'

Abhay thought for a few minutes. Finally, he said, 'You're right. I should not give up on myself. And I should not worry about what people will say. I have given it everything I can and if it's not enough, then I shouldn't keep trying.' Abhay smiled and then, looking into her eyes, he asked, 'How can you be so rational about such critical decisions in life?'

Juhi couldn't control her laughter hearing that. 'It wouldn't be appropriate to compare you with me, but even my mom never wanted me to come to Pune to work. She had her own reasons—like girls from a small towns should not think about careers and should have no ambitions. If it were in her hands, I would have never come this far. After returning home, I struggled with my own demons. To not get what you want shatters you. For months, I was heartbroken and couldn't see any way ahead. But I believed in myself and my father explained things to me the way I am explaining it to you. Today will be your past in the future, and it's you who have to decide how you want to look back at it. Because being unhappy is only half a life, and how long can you go on living with that as your reality? Five years? Ten? Thirty? Don't you deserve more?'

Abhay nodded. 'I don't know how to thank you.'

'Don't thank me. Thank your conscience for guiding you and taking you on the right path.' Juhi smiled.

Abhay could see the way ahead clearly now. He had broken all the barriers in his mind. He was choosing to live his life. He didn't want to get into a debate of whether he was right or wrong. He just placed his own happiness above all the rest of the complexities of life.

• •

We are all on the quest of discovering ourselves, day after day, desperate to recognise our worth. At times Juhi had felt moments of immense fulfilment, and at times she had felt she just couldn't go on. But for the sake of her own happiness, she stayed strong.

When she landed in Bhopal, she went to the investment firm that Suyash had been in touch with and gave them all the necessary documentation from Rohit. The firm representative had already cleared the formalities and was just waiting for this paperwork. Delighted, she closed the deal and returned home where she gave everyone the good news. Her father had tears of happiness in his eyes.

'Congratulations, beta, I knew you would not let me down. More than that, you will never let your own self down. You had that spark in your eyes that made me believe that you would achieve what you want on your own. And looking at you now, I can proudly say that I was right.'

'It's all because of you, Papa. You are my inspiration.' Juhi wiped his tears.

'No, it's because of your hard work.' Juhi's father held her by her shoulders. 'The way you handle little adversities impresses me. How you cope with being told you can't do something is inspiring. You've already proven to me that you're everything I wished you'd be.'

Juhi's eyes searched for her mother who, after hearing the news, had walked inside her room.

'Is Maa not happy?' she asked her father.

'Why do you think that? She was extremely happy when you had called to inform that the deal is done,' he said, and then asked her to go and have a word with her mother.

Slowly, she disentangled herself from his arms and walked up to her mother in her room. She was messaging someone on her mobile. When she heard Juhi's footsteps, she looked up.

'What happened, Maa? Are you still upset with me?' Juhi sat beside her on the bed.

'I am upset with myself,' her mother said with a heavy heart. She held Juhi's hands. 'I am sorry, I always told you to live like I have lived. I always asked you to do only what is expected from girls in our small-town culture. I am sorry about that. I know you would have blamed me many times, but I was afraid. I was scared for you. You'll understand only when you have a child. I do not doubt your judgement and capabilities, but worrying is a part of my job as a mother.'

'Maa, I am not blaming you at all. I was thinking about it while returning from Pune this time, that if that resistance hadn't been there, then the zeal to prove things to you and myself wouldn't have developed in me. So, please don't be sorry.'

'You know what, Juhi,' her mother said as she held her shoulders and kissed her forehead. 'Today, I am proud of you. Today I am proud that you did things on your own terms and went down a path of your choosing. Today I am proud that you didn't surrender to the life a girl is expected to live in our family.'

Juhi broke down hearing that. She had always longed to hear these words from her mother. For years, she had wanted that appreciation from her mother. What she couldn't achieve from years of working in Pune, she had managed to do in her town, on her own. Her mom embraced her with joy. Juhi got up and drank a glass of water to calm down.

'Maa, you always asked me to get married and I told you that I am not ready.' She turned towards her mom, who looked at her keenly. 'I felt the time was not right. You know I was going through a very rough phase and then wanted to take Happy Cows to a particular level. But now I feel that, by next year, I am okay to get married. So you can look for someone you feel is appropriate.'

Juhi's mom said, 'No, I was wrong that time, and now I won't come to an emotional conclusion. Honestly, I feel even now the time isn't right. Happy Cows has just started growing and you should totally focus on it. You have got a big deal and it's your responsibility now to live up to the expectations; there will be so many hurdles that you will have to overcome.'

Juhi was shocked. 'Maa, you are saying no to marriage? Am I dreaming?'

Her mother laughed. 'I even messaged all the ladies in the group that my daughter is expanding Happy Cows and has got a huge new deal. They replied that your daughter is taking a responsibility like a son should and I clearly told them that she is my daughter and I'm proud of her.' Her mother held her hand affectionately and said, 'Do what your heart wants. We are there right by your side.'

I feel the happiest today, like I am on top of this universe. More than anything, I could make my mom proud, my parents proud, what else do I want? One decision changed the course of my life. I was not sure when I moved away from Pune if I was doing the right thing. But now I know it was. It was that one moment when I had to decide and then stick with it. Papa has always pushed me to levels I didn't even know existed. He always said, 'It's okay to be sad, you can let yourself feel sad for a while, but you have to, have to, pick yourself up and show up even though you don't want to. Go do something and force yourself to feel better, and eventually you will.'

••

The same day that he met Juhi, Abhay told Karan he would be accepting the Singapore project. He asked Karan to begin the visa formalities. He didn't inform anyone about it, not even Stuti. He wasn't sure what he would do once he got there. He still hoped that, with time, Stuti would understand his importance in her life and things would get back to normal. But for now, he needed to work on his worth more than anything else.

After a couple of days, when all the formalities were finally done and he had an early morning flight to catch the next day, he messaged Juhi.

'I am leaving finally. I have an early morning flight; had asked for it purposely so that I can leave when Stuti is asleep. All I wanted to say was THANK YOU ONCE AGAIN for believing me and reminding me about what I am capable of.'

Juhi was in a discussion with the technicians and workers she had taken on contract to expand her farm. She read Abhay's message after some time and was happy that he had eventually taken charge of his life. She felt bad he had to leave his son behind, but she also felt maybe that was the only way he could discover himself.

'That's great. All the best for the new start. I am sure you are having a tough time but I know you are strong enough to handle it. Take care.'

Abhay read the message and replied, 'I promise that I'll visit your farm once.' He took a deep breath and a smile appeared on his face rereading the message. He added a smiling emoji and sent it.

Juhi was right. It wasn't easy, it never is. To leave where you belong and start afresh, to leave the ones you love and imagined that you would spend your entire life with. But at times, that is what you need to do.

Abhay spent the entire evening with Ameya and each memory of his with him made him emotional. Later, he had dinner with Stuti, and then when they were in their room, Abhay went to her and gave her a hug.

'What happened? You are suddenly more affectionate than normal,' she said.

'It's just … I feel …' Abhay didn't know what to say. 'Nothing. You know what, I just wanted to say I'll always love you.'

Abhay lay down on his side of the bed, and soon his pillow was soaked with his tears. When Stuti was asleep, he turned around and gazed at her for some time. All those days when they had really loved each other played on his mind. He gently ran his hand through her hair and kissed her forehead. Finally, he got up, changed his clothes and looked at both his wife and son for one last time. Leaving the room with a heavy heart, he placed the letter he had written on the dining table.

When you wake up, you'll find this letter, but not me. I know I should have told you, but I also know what you would have said. And that you would have found a way to stop me from leaving.

Stuti, I love you, but this relationship has turned toxic and it's breaking me. I am sorry, but I can't let that happen. I'm finally moving on. At one point you were my world, beautiful and full of wonders. But now you no longer have any interest in anything other than your work. You are uninterested in my job, in my thoughts; you treat me like I am intellectually inferior. At night, we lie side by side, yet you still don't hear me crying.

I don't cry myself to sleep anymore, my tears don't get me anywhere, no one can hear. I hated waiting for something that I feared wasn't going to happen. And I hated myself even more for being right. All I want is to be held, to be told I am appreciated, to enjoy life's simple adventures with the woman I wanted to share my life and my world with.

I am scared that Ameya is being raised in a world where snapping at each other is acceptable communication, a world where love isn't everyone's priority. Your approach to life is the antithesis of mine. I want to laugh until it hurts; I don't remember the last time you laughed. I want to run into your arms when you come home, and I want you to run into mine. I want to share the load. The slightest touch that speaks volumes, a kiss on the neck—it induces the saddest feeling within me simply because I know that you will never do that to me. I need moments like those; they should be my fuel, rather than the anger that now replaces the love that once was. I am so sad. For you. For me. For Ameya. For the life that we were meant to have together. But I can't stay for the sake of Ameya; I know it would only prolong an increasingly unbearable agony. I always thought I was unbreakable, but continuing down this road will surely break me. So, this time, instead of chasing after a happiness that we're just not going to find together, let's end things now. I am going back to being the man I was before. I want to revive the man that I used to be. He was fearless, independent and gave zero fucks about other people who would bring him down.

I'm truly sorry for the pain this will cause you. I feel bad, and believe me, it's not going to be easy for me either. I really wish things didn't have to be this way, but it just won't work. Someday, I know, you'll agree that it was the best thing for both of us. Whatever happens, I wish you well. You truly do deserve the best. Please take care of yourself and Ameya. Give him the time he needs. Please know that I do love you, and a part of me always will. But sometimes just love isn't enough.

• •

Abhay's journey wasn't so much about becoming anything. It was more about unbecoming everything that wasn't really him so he could be who he was meant to be in the first place. Everyone comes to a moment in their lives when they have to choose between their own happiness or continue to live in the circumstances they are in. This was Abhay's moment. To decide whether what he did was right or wrong is not as easy as differentiating between black and white. Things in life are never just white and black. Like Juhi had said, 'Sometimes it's not about choosing between right and wrong, but choosing the better of the wrong choices.'

When Stuti read the letter, she panicked and tried calling Abhay, but his phone was not reachable.

In Singapore, Abhay had taken a few days to settle into the apartment given to him by the company. He didn't give his Singapore number to anyone from his family. Later, when he got in touch with Stuti, she exploded, but didn't agree to shift even when she calmed down. Her ego had burned her family life, and like they say, ego and love cannot exist together. Abhay asked her to give it some time—maybe a few months or years to their own selves to contemplate whether they really needed each other's presence in their lives. He was still a father and had decided to take all the responsibility of Ameya. But sometimes, in a relationship, two people simply outgrow each other. Holding on is not always a sign of strength. And letting go doesn't mean that you don't care. It's just realising that you can't control anyone, only yourself.

For Juhi, she didn't get her love. She kept falling in love with the thought of Abhay loving her back, but she got to meet her real self on the way. She had started to hate herself after finding out Abhay was in a relationship. She had always relied on other people to get her out of tough situations, but it was only when she found the answers within that her true journey began. She successfully expanded her farm and was able to get more than the expected purchase order after a few weeks as the demand increased substantially. The brand made her products available in all the stores in the vicinity and in the next few months she made a plan to open another farm for the western region and was in touch with Rohit regarding this.

She still sometimes remembers Abhay's words, that she will never get what she wants. All she wanted at that time was his love. But not getting what you want is sometimes a great stroke of luck. Isn't it? She would never have found her true potential otherwise.

In the meanwhile, she also completed writing her novel and read out the final lines of it to Nisha on a call.

When I look back, I can say that you gave words to the voice inside my head. Words that made me realise I was much stronger than I gave myself credit for. The hurt caused by you allowed me to explore new things, and I thank you for that. Thank you for setting me free from something that could have become comfortable and made me complacent, when big dreams and adventures were meant to be had. Thank you for making me see the beauty in this breakdown. But that certainly wasn't how I wanted to end my story and I decided to pen one down. It wouldn't have been possible without you. I know that every part of me will forever feel grateful that you didn't love me back, that you broke my heart and showed me what I'm really made of. I realised that there is a time and place for certain people to come into your life. There is also a reason why it doesn't always last forever. I never understood hating a significant other ... you were once a very important piece of my life and, looking back, a big piece of the puzzle to make up my life today. Thank you for allowing me to fall, to express the deepest of human emotions and connect with another person on that level. Despite the outcome, I am proud that I allowed myself to experience those emotions—

the good and the bad. I may have failed in a one-sided love affair but I gained individuality, opportunity and the confidence to be something in life instead.

Most importantly, thank you for giving me the opportunity to strengthen the best and longest relationship I've ever had—the one with myself. I chose not to break down, I chose to live ... this may be the end of the story, but my life has just begun!

ALSO BY SUDEEP NAGARKAR

On the eve of her twenty-fifth birthday, Ruhi's family and friends throw her a surprise party. The next morning, she is found lying on the floor of her room, dead. Her brother Kartik is convinced she was murdered. But no one believes him.

The police investigation concludes that it is a case of suicide. Kartik is devastated and suffers an emotional breakdown. Not only is his beloved little sister gone, but there is no one who will believe his story. His elder sister, Dipika, is convinced he is crazy, a drunkard who doesn't know what's happening around him. Ruhi's heartbroken boyfriend Mihir thinks Kartik's love for his sister is blinding him. However, Kartik is sure he actually saw the killer, even though he has no clear memory of what happened that night.

Seven months later, Kartik is released from a treatment centre and Dipika dedicates herself to helping him restart his life. But Kartik can only focus on finding out what really happened. He is determined to bring justice to Ruhi.

Can Kartik uncover the truth when everyone's a suspect—including himself? *Stand By Me!* is an emotion-charged, intricate thriller, and the story of a brother who pushes himself beyond all limits for the love of his sister.

Relationships require openness, and that brings vulnerability. If you open up, you risk getting hurt; if you don't, you may never know the relationship you deserve.

Disha has always been shy and wary, and finds it difficult to make friends. Having grown up with parents who bicker all the time, she craves warmth and harmony. And ever since she first experienced the emotion of love, she has longed to be the centre of a special someone's world. But with every fibre of her being, Disha believes she is unlucky in love. The hardest part for anyone is finding the 'right' person—but in her search for that man, broken hearts and broken promises is all she's had.

With no luck and no one on the horizon, Disha gives up and agrees to an arranged marriage. Is true love not written in her stars? Will she be able to reverse her fortunes, or is she destined to never find her soulmate?

A Second Chance is the heart-wrenching story of a multifaceted girl and her search to find the love she deserves.